OPPOSED DESIRES

KATHERINE MCINTYRE

HOT TREE PUBLISHING

OPPOSED DESIRES

REHOBOTH PACT #2

KATHERINE MCINTYRE

HOT TREE PUBLISHING

Opposed Desires © 2021 by Katherine McIntyre

Opposed Desires is a work of fiction. All names, characters, events and places found therein are either from the author's imagination or used fictitiously. Any similarity to persons alive or dead, actual events, locations, or organizations is entirely coincidental and not intended by the author.

For information, contact the publisher, Hot Tree Publishing.

www.hottreepublishing.com

Editing: Hot Tree Editing

Cover Designer: BookSmith Design

E-book ISBN: 978-1-922359-94-0

Paperback ISBN: 978-1-922359-95-7

ALSO BY KATHERINE MCINTYRE

Rehoboth Pact

Confined Desires

Opposed Desires

Restrained Desires

Chesapeake Days

Stronger Than Hope

Stronger Than Passion

Outlaws

Midnight Heist

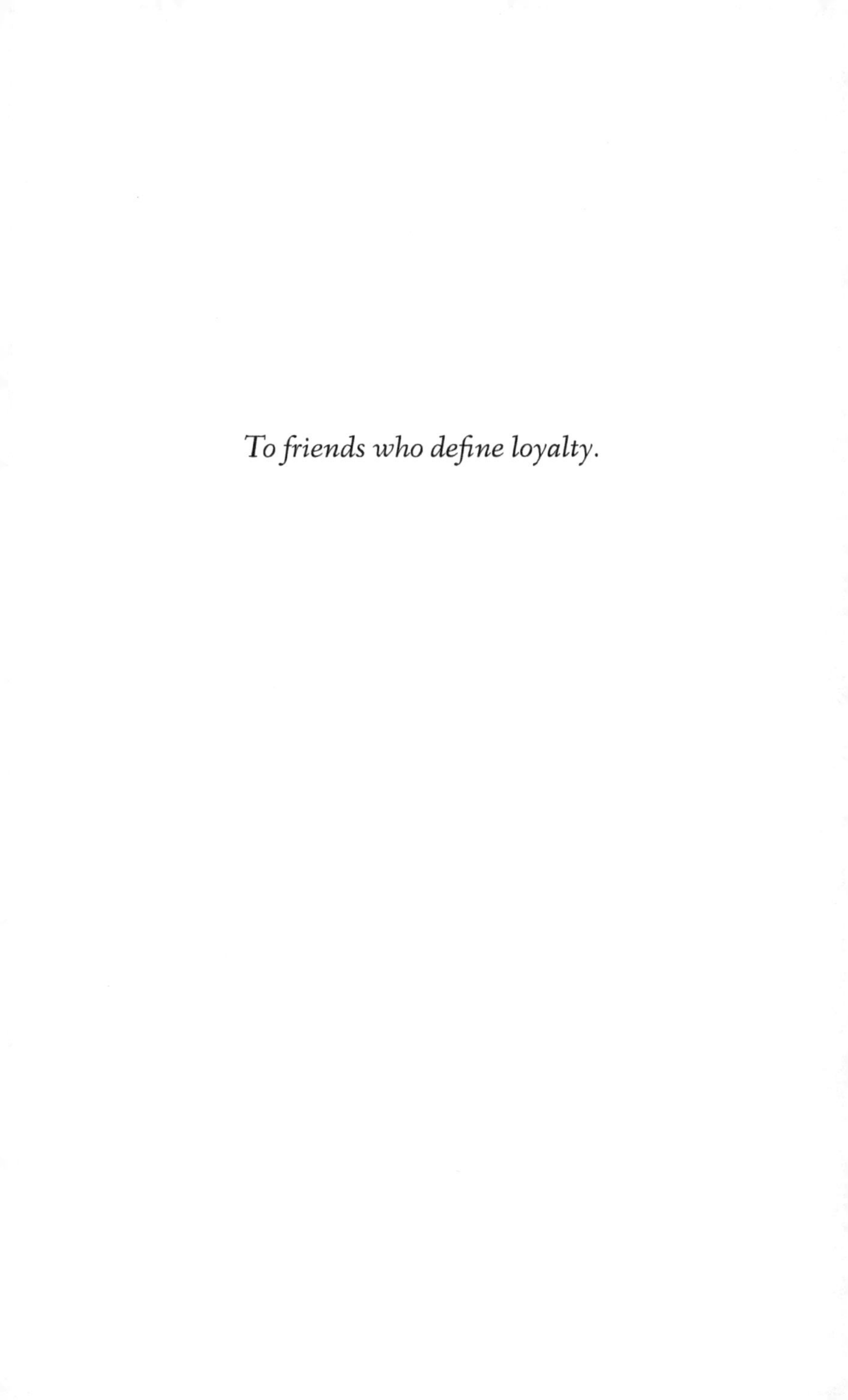

To friends who define loyalty.

CHAPTER ONE

The shore was packed tighter than a gym in the beginning of January.

Aubrey strode down the weathered slats of the boardwalk, dodging folks with every half step. Not like she gave a damn. The midday sun was piping hot overhead, the scents of salty fries and pizza sizzled in the air, and the women strolling to the beach were even more scorching.

Summer in Rehoboth wasn't just tradition—it was sacred between her, Kyle, and Sky. Though this year, Sky had to spoil their fun by finding true love and all that jazz. Now Aubrey and Kyle formed the singles party. Not like her bed stayed empty often though. Sweat dripped down the side of her face, the sticky droplets tickling as they crawled. Her stomach rumbled at the smell of stalls that served everything from crispy funnel cake to sweet, cool custard, but she gripped her bags a little tighter and passed them by. She'd been sent on a very important mission to grab booze for the rental, and she wouldn't let the girls down.

She reached the edge of the boardwalk and squinted at the maze of streets that spread out into a mix of residential and businesses. Their road was visible from here. They booked their rental a year in advance because it was right near the water. Aubrey might rebel against anything resembling commitment regarding relationships, but she dug her routines, whether they be the jab, cross, and uppercuts she taught at the gym or the yearly trip she took with her best friends.

The seaside breeze swept by, and she drew in a deep inhale, all salt and ozone. She wove to their side street, the purple shutters of their rental standing out at the end of the block. The booze she'd picked up strained the handles of the bag, an assortment of rum, more rum, gin, and whisky to appease Sky and Kyle. If it had been up to her, she would've replaced the bottles with more Captain Jack.

She neared the house that was hers for the week, the perfect place to unwind and get away from everything. She needed the escape from her status quo too. Work had been slammed, and as of late, the whole trolling for hot women at bars had lost that gilt thrill, especially the more she watched how gooey sweet Sky and her girlfriend were together. Chels had been complaining about her husband, Noah, more than ever, and every time she visited her folks, Dad asked Aubs when she would bring home a husband.

Next time to never, Pops.

When she'd come out at the tender age of sixteen, Mom had been the supportive one, whereas Dad played the "Don't Ask, Don't Tell" game.

She slowed as she closed in on the last few houses on the way to hers. They all possessed their own unique charm—bright colored shutters and wide porches with wicker furniture. The languid spell of this area grew infectious, a sleepy beach town by day that knew how to party at night. Even though Rehoboth only lay an hour and a half from their hometown in Wilmington, it felt like a time zone away. Her gaze glided over the house next to theirs, and she almost tripped.

Selina Beckett sat on one of the wicker benches on the porch of the house beside theirs, her feet propped up and her nose buried in a book.

"Of all the gin joints in all the towns in all the world," Aubs called out as she came to a stop and rerouted her steps to Selina's direction. She should keep walking—Selina was the owner of Renegades, the hottest queer bar in Wilmington, and she had threatened to ban Aubrey almost a dozen times. But Aubrey couldn't deny that any challenge thrilled her, and the tougher the woman was, the more she got inspired to ram those walls down.

Y'know, until the eventuality when they hooked up and Aubrey ghosted. Because she was chickenshit on her best day. That would never happen with Selina. The woman loathed her.

All the more reason to annoy her now.

Aubrey's feet creaked on the steps of Selina's porch as she approached. The woman placed her book on her lap to look at her.

Selina Beckett normally dressed in a mixture of sophisti-goth and punk when she worked at the bar, with Wiccan charms around her neck and wrists, but today she wore a pale off-the-shoulder tee with the black straps of a sports bra poking out and a pair of maroon leggings underneath that came to mid-calf.

She arched an elegant eyebrow. "What are you doing here, Aubrey?" The bright sunlight illumi-nated the copper in her skin, making her dark eyes and her relaxed black pixie cut stand out even more. The woman's sensual lips told a story with each quirk, everything about her a mixture of mysterious, sultry, and cutting.

"We're staying next door for the week, Selina," she said, elongating her full name. "Looks like we'll be neighbors."

Selina stared at the ceiling of the porch. "Goddess, what did I do to deserve this punishment?"

"Maybe she heard you were a little masochistic," Aubs teased, her voice growing husky. Nothing thrilled her more than watching the woman's irritation grow.

"Maybe she's trying to teach me patience," Selina shot back. "Are you going to have the normal pussy parade coming through? Make sure to keep it down in the late hours—I like getting sleep on vacation."

"I can't help if the ladies are enjoying themselves," Aubs said with a wink. "I like my partners to leave satisfied."

"How long do you let the bedsheets cool before you send them out on their ass, Aubrey?" she asked, that reproachful gaze devouring her. "An hour? Five minutes? We both know they don't stay all night."

Aubs placed her hands on her hips. "Do I look

like a cuddler to you? They'll be more comfortable in their own beds rather than mine. I'm just being considerate."

"Why don't you take all your bountiful consideration and head on over to your rental?" Selina responded with the same smooth coolness as always. "I was in the middle of a good scene."

Aubs parked herself on the arm of Selina's wicker seat, which creaked under her weight. Selina grimaced, and Aubs's grin widened as she peeked at the cover with a couple clutching one another.

"I took you for more of the thriller or serial killer type of read, not romance," Aubs proclaimed, her teeth poking out of her smile. "Don't tell me you're a secret softie?"

Selina shot her a pointed look. "The romance is fiction, but if you want to experience a thriller, keep bothering me on my porch while I'm trying to read."

"Tantalizing," Aubs said, grinning as she hopped from her perch and strode toward the steps. "Looking forward to seeing you around town, gorgeous."

Selina's silence answered back, and amusement welled in Aubrey's chest. She'd been annoying the woman for years, to the point that it'd become an art form. And still, Selina had never cracked. The temporary thrill offered some color on a canvas that had grown pretty monochromatic as of late.

Aubs headed up to the front door of their rental, hearing the murmur of voices from inside.

Escape. That's what this week revolved around, and goddamn, she needed it more than ever.

LOUD CHATTER ECHOED TO THE RAFTERS OF Castaway Cantina, which was as packed as the beaches had been during the day. Not like Aubrey minded—they'd been able to snag a table for their crew, and the margaritas were flowing. The cedar floors, walls, and ceiling leant themselves to the beach vibe, as did the wide-open windows that the salt breeze wafted through. Electronica pulsed from the speakers, and a good mix of people of all spectrums of the rainbow stopped in this watering hole. Aubs leaned back into the booth, stretching one arm over Kyle's shoulders.

Her best friend had stuck with her since she moved to the area at the end of high school, and onward into college. She'd knock out anyone who tried to fuck with her Ky. The woman was all short auburn hair, a cheeky smile that turned shy more often than not, and a narrow nose and dimples that added to her preciousness. Adorable, but Aubs had always viewed her as a sister rather than a lover.

Across the booth from them sat Mia and Sky, wrapped up in their new couple bliss. Mia looked scoop-of-sundae gorgeous with her long brown waves pulled back and a breezy teal dress on. She leaned against Sky, who'd dressed up for the occasion in a thin tee and jean shorts. Truth be told, they made a stunning couple, and Aubs couldn't be happier Sky had gotten her head out of her ass to make that shit serious.

Between Ky's crippling self-esteem issues, Aubrey's own rebellion problems that resulted in a hefty case of anti-commitment, and Sky's avoidance of all emotional conversations, they'd been a train about to derail. At least one of them jumped off in time—Aubrey and Ky still sped straight ahead toward one gangbusters collision.

"I'm shocked you're here with us," Sky drawled. "Haven't you found some foxy babe who needs tending to?"

"I sure will," Aubrey responded, revealing teeth with her grin. "Once I finish this margarita." She took a sip, the tartness of the lime, the bite of tequila, and the salt from the rim all mingling into a delicious mouthful.

Ky let out a hefty sigh into her margarita and narrowed her eyes, scanning the bar. "How do you even approach anyone? I get so tongue-tied, and no one finds the question 'Would you rather be buried or cremated when you die?' charming."

Aubs let out a snort. "Sweetie, you're going to want to retire that one."

"Once. I said it once. The rest of the things I blurt out aren't much better," Ky said, imprinting her forehead on the table.

"Why don't you lead with what you do for a living?" Mia asked. "The second women find out you're a massage therapist, they'll probably flip."

Ky gave her a weary glance. "Yeah, at least until I tell them their rhomboids are overstretched and their sternocleidomastoids are as well due to forward head posture." She glanced in Aubrey's direction. "How the hell do you do it?"

Aubs snorted. "Hon, I'm too much of a dumbass to be awkward. Your problem is you let your mind get in the way, whereas I let my body do the talking. A few questions about them, a couple of loaded glances, and usually that's game, set, match."

"We can't all be kickboxers with crazy abs,

Aubs," Sky shot back. She glanced at Ky. "Don't worry, I'm just as shitty at talking to women. I got lucky enough to reel this one in years ago."

Aubs took another sip from her margarita, scanning the women by the bar. Some of the ladies seemed to already be coupled up, leaning in close to each other, holding hands, or just having the cozy vibe that tended to coincide with commitment. She wasn't searching for any of those. On the other end of the bar, she caught sight of Selina perched on one of the wooden stools beside a few other familiar faces from Renegades. This time, the woman wore her normal shades of goth: black cigarette pants, a gray shirt that showcased a stunning rack, and a flare of red from the bandanna wrapped around her head.

The temptation to march over and bother her reared up in a big way, but then Aubrey'd get sucked too far in to bag herself a fling for the night. Aubs drank down another slurp of the tart sweetness of her drink and continued scanning the bar for some unattached hotties. Summertime at the beach meant most folks searched for the same thing she did—some feel-good, NSA enjoyment.

Her gaze landed on a skinny blonde who sat by herself nursing a glass of red wine. Once in a while, the woman would look toward the door, but for the most part, she seemed content to chat with the bartender. With her heartbreaker blue eyes and wearing a flirty pink dress that came to mid-thigh, she came across as a little more Barbie than Aubs went for, but hey, a different flavor each night couldn't hurt.

Aubs placed her glass on the table, drawing Ky's attention, who'd been in mid-conversation with Mia while they discussed awkward moments on dates.

"Uh oh, looks like she's locked and loaded on a target," Sky teased from across the table. Her eyes crinkled in amusement.

Aubs flipped her the finger. "I'll be back, ladies."

She straightened up and strode away from the booth. She tugged at the bottom of her loose-fitting white tank that revealed her black sports bra where the armholes were deeply cut. She'd chosen her red shorts because they hugged her ass in exactly the right way. The closer she got, the more she studied the other woman. Her mouth was pensive, eyes distant, and she nursed the wine like it owed her money. Fresh out of a relationship, maybe?

Aubrey's phone buzzed, and she glanced at the screen. Chels.

She should be avoiding these calls on vacation, but she had a hard time denying her little sis anything. Aubs snapped the phone to her ear, stopping mid-stride. She leaned against the side of the bar.

"Make it quick, Chels," she said. "Hard to hear right now."

"Look, Mom and Dad didn't want me to say anything, but I figured you should know," Chelsea started.

The seriousness in Chelsea's voice was the only tipoff she needed. Aubrey made a quick reroute, heading toward the door. She hoped the girls weren't watching, because she wanted to deal with this shit in peace—whatever the news might be. The sinking in her stomach had reached Titanic levels by the time she stepped outside into the night air. Only a few folks lingered outside smoking cigarettes, the heavy scent lingering around the entrance. She found a spot a few feet away and slumped to the ground.

"All right. Hit me with it," she said, forcing her voice to stay steady.

"Dad took Mom to the hospital earlier today because she passed out. They're running tests, and nothing's come up yet, so they didn't want to worry you while you were on vacation."

"Yeah, I'd rather know how Mom's doing," Aubs

said, a sickness washing over her like she'd suddenly vaulted back four years ago to when Mom had first gotten diagnosed with thyroid cancer. Back to the fear that had swirled through her and consumed her entire family, like one by one they'd get dragged into shark-infested waters.

"I know," Chels said, the same concern tugging at her voice. "No need to rush home though. Those assholes aren't even letting me go over and visit. I promise I'll keep you in the loop either way."

"Thanks, sis," Aubs murmured, trying to ignore the thump, thump, thump of her heart. "Have a good night."

"You too," she responded and hung up.

After the line went silent, Aubs sagged against the wall. She tilted her head to look at the night sky, unable to stop the dizzying swirl of panic as it descended. The struggle had been nasty: feeding tubes, vomiting, and watching the pounds just drop off of Mom. Her mother barely made it out alive.

Not again.

A scuff sounded beside her, and the fumes of cigarette smoke followed, tickling her nose.

"Not trying to cramp your style," a familiar voice said. "Just looking for a clear spot to smoke."

Aubrey looked up to see Selina standing beside her.

Of course. The woman who made cool and unaffected look like an art form. The last person on earth Aubrey wanted seeing her mid-breakdown.

CHAPTER TWO

Selina sucked down the first drag of nicotine, her whole body relaxing as it hit her system. The crowds shouldn't bother her since she was a bar owner and all, but she was used to having the buffer of the bar to keep from the elbow jabs and random jostling that happened on the opposite side. She cast a glance to her left, unable to help herself.

Aubrey Moore crouched there as if she didn't hear a word she said. Fine by her. The woman was a cocked pistol of trouble on the best days, and in a party environment like summertime in Rehoboth, Selina was shocked the woman loitered out here rather than seducing some lonesome hottie at the bar.

Just like Aubrey did time and time again at

Renegades. First day she'd met Aubrey Moore, she'd been struck by her Guatemalan good looks—tanned, smooth skin, curious dark eyes, and a smile that gave whiplash. Yet she'd watched over the years as Aubrey added notch after notch to her bedpost, charming women by the barstools and leaving with them before an hour passed. Honestly, the chase seemed exhausting, and all that the pattern cemented in Selina's mind was "avoid at all costs."

Not like she hadn't looked though. Even now, the woman was the sort of scorching to turn heads. She kept her hair pulled back in a ponytail on a permanent basis, tonight no exception, and the exercise outfits she donned left little to the imagination of how in shape she was.

"Fuck me," Aubrey said, scrubbing her face with her palms.

"Not even if you begged, sweetheart," Selina responded on instinct, unable to help the retorts that popped from her lips around this woman.

"Hilarious," Aubrey responded, her voice saltine dry.

Selina took another drag from her cigarette. Clearly, Aubrey was struggling with something, but Selina wasn't about to go digging around in other people's business. She'd learned early on from owning a bar to keep the conversation superficial and light—save the real stuff for those in her inner circle. Aubrey grew quiet, staring at her beat-up Adidas. There was something vulnerable in the crouch though, something that caused Selina's gaze to return.

"You look like you need a cigarette," Selina murmured, nudging the pack her way in offering. Goddess above, entertaining a conversation with Aubrey wasn't a good plan. A good plan would be heading back into the bar with Cass and Steph, even though she wasn't feeling the party-by-the-beach scene tonight.

"Nah, I don't smoke," Aubrey said, casting a glance at the bar. "Fuck me, I don't want to go back in."

"Did you already strike out with whoever was your pick of the night?" Selina asked, not knowing why she was humoring her. Maybe it was the hope-less look in Aubrey's chocolate eyes as their gazes locked. It was nothing she'd ever seen before from the woman who appeared to be all slick smiles and cockiness.

"Didn't even get the chance," Aubrey said, tugging on the end of her ponytail. She glanced at the entrance of Castaway Cantina again. "This is a little crazy, and guaranteed you're going to say no, but do you want to get out of here? Not a line, like... a walk on the beach or something?"

Truth be told, yeah, she wanted to get away from the crowds and soak in the quiet. Just not with the biggest player on the Delaware Beaches.

Aubrey scrubbed at her face again. "Right, forget I said anything. It's just the first night here, and I don't want to go back in and ruin everyone's good time. And hey, you can't stand me, so at least my bullshit won't affect you."

"What bullshit?" Selina asked, keeping her tone level. Still, she couldn't help her piqued curiosity. Something was off with the woman she normally swapped casual insults with.

"Mom's in the hospital, and they're running tests, so, yeah. Might be nothing. But it might also mean her cancer's returned." Aubrey's lip trembled, and her gaze darted away, as if to stop Selina from catching the glossiness in her eyes. "Sorry, fuck. That isn't the type of thing you unload on someone at random."

"I'm not exactly a stranger," Selina responded. The storm cloud made sense now. Aubrey pushed up from her crouch as if she might stride off in the next few moments. She chewed on her lip. If this was normal Aubrey Moore, Selina would head right back inside. The woman's usual ego could fill an amphitheater. However, right now, a different person stood before her looking for help, and damn, escaping to the beach sounded like a solid plan.

Selina stuck out her hand. "Truce," she said. "Tonight only."

Aubrey cocked a brow, looking at the offending hand with hesitation. She pressed her lips together and slapped her palm against Selina's. "Truce."

Selina dropped her cig to the ground and crushed it under her heel before grabbing the stub and flicking it to the nearest ashtray. She glanced toward Aubrey who still stood in the same spot. "So, are you coming?"

Aubrey walked in stride with her as they headed in the direction of the ocean, not a far stroll from the hubbub and roar of the busy boardwalk. Castaway Cantina was one of the bars a few blocks away from the beach, so they'd be able to escape the alcohol and crowd-induced noise within minutes.

They strode in silence, dodging past the drunks swaying along the streets, their loud, slurred laughter echoing in the air. Selina found the quiet, in and of itself, a shock. She'd never been in Aubrey's presence for five minutes without the woman trying to make a pass or offering up some flirty comment. When Selina had maneuvered around her advances for years, Aubrey switched to incessant teasing, as if she couldn't take being ignored. Selina racked her brain for topics, yet in the end, clung to her silence. If Aubrey wanted to talk about the situation, she could, but Selina wasn't the type to push.

She fired off a quick text to Cass, letting her know she headed back to the house early. Not like anyone would be surprised. For someone who owned and operated a bar, she rarely went to one herself. Felt too much like being at work.

They reached the edge of the boardwalk, the sand and the sea stretching before them in a pale strip that clashed with the inky darkness of the waters. Something loosened in Selina's chest at the sight. The ocean always calmed her, especially at night when most of the daytime rabble had retreated. She was used to being surrounded by people, but sometimes she preferred the solitude.

"I'm sorry for dragging you away from your friends," Aubrey said, loosening her ponytail to run her fingers through her hair. The moonlight high-lighted her deep brown strands, and the way they fell down to her shoulders made her seem a little softer than the sharp, pointed woman Selina'd come to know. She found this side of Aubrey far more alluring.

"I could've done this by myself," Aubrey admitted. "I just lost my mind a little bit back there."

"I wouldn't have left if I didn't want to." Selina shrugged. "Bars aren't really my scene."

"Said the bar owner." Aubrey gave her the side-eye. "Why even own one then?"

Selina swung her arms by her side, staring at the half moon overhead. It glowed with pearlescent promise, a steadiness she'd always longed for. "Spend your whole life traveling from one town to the next and you get desperate to set down roots. I wanted to create a safe space for folks like me, and I needed to stay in one place. Renegades ensured that."

Aubrey shook her head, a throaty laugh escaping her. "I've known you for four years now, and I'm pretty sure that's the most you've ever shared about yourself."

"Well, we're having a truce tonight," Selina said. "Tomorrow I can go back to loathing you, and we can return to the usual witty repartee."

Aubrey pointed at herself. "Me? Witty? Glad you think so, doll. I don't keep track of half of the things that leave my mouth."

"Good to know," Selina murmured, a smile

nudging her lips. The earnest note in Aubrey's voice had her warming up to the woman far faster than she had in years. The lack of an agenda helped too. Selina slipped off her sandals to hold them in her hand, walking barefoot on the sandy shore. "Won't the girls be wondering where you went?"

Aubrey shrugged. "They'll assume I took someone home. It's my MO when I pull the vanishing act."

"That sounds pretty lonesome." The words slipped out before she could help herself. Selina licked her lips, not knowing what to say. The salt air wove past her, caressing her senses.

"Different bed every night? How could that be lonely?" Aubrey joked, yet her voice scraped over the words like a tire crunching uneven rocks. She cast Selina a sideways glance. "Maybe a little," she admitted, her dark eyes somber in the surrounding dark. The slight gleam from the moonlight only enhanced that sharp, vibrant beauty. This version of the woman, framed by moonlight and unguarded, with her hair down, struck Selina as far more gorgeous than the sweet-talker she regularly saw at the bar.

Aubrey bent down to slide off her sneakers, and Selina couldn't help but follow the motion. Those long legs were on full display, all corded muscle and defined calves, and the red shorts she wore show-cased a gorgeous sculpted ass. Selina never argued that the woman was hot—Aubrey Moore undeni-ably, unequivocally raised her temperature, but she was also the exact sort of person Selina needed to avoid.

She wanted someone to settle down with. Someone who wouldn't get bored, or cheat, or ditch her when the routine got too monotonous. Been there, done that. She'd learned her lessons well and committed them to heart.

Aubrey straightened up with her shoes in one hand, and an honest smile blossomed on her face. "That's a bit better. Let's go dip our feet in the water."

Selina shook her head, her heart beating a little faster. "Sure, and we can get dragged away by the kraken lurking in the deep while we're at it."

Aubrey started heading in the direction of the tides, which glittered under the silvery moonlight. The gentle glow, the rocking ebb and flow of the water, and the soothing sounds of the waves crashing to the shore all surrounded her like a cocoon. Selina felt like she'd been transported to a different realm, far away from the lights and crowds on the board-walk. She approached the edge where Aubrey waited for her to catch up, the tide kissing the shore again and again and again.

A shiver rolled down her spine as she crept closer, the sand growing damp beneath her feet. The ocean beyond appeared black with wicked crests, a wild, churning morass that seemed tranquil and like a void in the same breath.

Aubrey took a few steps forward until the water rolled around her feet and her ankles, and then she glanced back. "Are you coming?"

Selina hesitated. She loved being by the ocean, but in it was another thing. She pursed her lips together and took a single step forward. If the water lapped her toes, she'd be fine. Still, a chill permeated through her, and she hadn't even stepped to the tide yet.

Aubrey turned around at this point, a grin lighting her features. "Are you afraid of the ocean, Selina Beckett?"

Selina skated a hand over her strands, avoiding Aubrey's gaze. "I prefer deep bodies of water from a distance." Any time she got too close or stepped too far in, all she could remember was the tug, like she'd been tripped, the flurry of bubbles and thrashing limbs, and the salt and aluminum that filled her mouth, choking her nostrils.

Aubrey stalked to her side, her eyes dancing with curiosity. "Hey, I won't force you in or anything. If you want, we can go close enough for the water to lap over our feet—no more than ankle deep."

Selina glanced between Aubrey and the growling, consuming beast before her. Aubrey offered a hand, her grin softening, her expression genuine. Truthfully, Selina wanted to. The most she'd done in far too long was approach the shoreline and watch, darting back the moment the icy tide nipped toward her.

Selina placed her hand in Aubrey's, and together they took the first steps forward. Her heart beat a little faster, but she focused on the warmth of Aubrey's palm and her confident movements as they took careful steps into the breach of the ocean. The first wave slithered up the shore, the foamy water rolling over her toes. A gasp of delight warred with the urge to bolt the other way and run up to the dry, still-warm sand.

"Just a few more steps forward," Aubrey said, her voice encouraging, steady. "And then we'll stop."

Selina followed her, one step, then another, until the waves coated the tops of her feet. Her heart jackhammered in her ears, but she focused on trying to steady her breaths, bringing her gaze to rest on

Aubrey rather than the immense expanse they faced, which could whip her away at a moment's notice. The woman moved with a physical confidence bred from her job, but the soft grin on her face and the way her eyes glittered as she stared out at the ocean was full of a gentle excitement Selina had never expected to witness.

"And, we'll stop here," Aubrey said, coming to a halt. She squeezed Selina's hand in reassurance. Selina stood beside her and glanced down. Ankle deep. She hadn't gotten this far in years. Standing this close to Aubrey, she caught the scent of sage and lemon intermingling with the salt breezes. The water rocked around them with a lullaby's ebb and flow.

Aubrey stared out over the water, not letting go of her hand. "Last time Mom got cancer, she barely made it out alive. The struggle wasn't just a couple rounds in the ring, and the strain affected the whole family. It happened a little before I started showing up at Renegades." She sucked in a sharp breath. "I'm just... not sure if I'm ready to dive back into that battle all over again."

"Not like cancer's kind enough to politely knock on the door and offer the choice," Selina murmured. Her heart twisted at the thought of the fight Aubrey and her family must have weathered.

Aubrey's gaze shifted toward her, a half smile on her lips. "True. Kind of a presumptuous jerk that way. Anyway, I just wanted to explain the breakdown you had the misfortune of stumbling onto."

Selina shrugged. "You didn't need a justification. Sometimes life kicks you in the labia. We all hit those moments."

"I guess so." Aubrey shrugged. She didn't say anything after, but she didn't have to. Selina started to piece together a better picture of the woman who clung to her togetherness like she was impermeable. She'd gotten so drawn into studying Aubrey that she almost forgot they stood here ankle-deep in the ocean. The water swirled around her, droplets kissing her shins. Aubrey hadn't let go of her hand, and she took some comfort in that.

"I don't know about you, but my feet are starting to freeze. Want to keep walking along the shore?" Aubrey asked, tilting her head toward the sand.

"I think I can manage that," Selina said with a slow smile. If someone asked her where she'd be tonight, her guess would've been either at the bar or tucked away on the porch with another book. Not taking a beachside stroll with eternal flirt and womanizer, Aubrey Moore. However, once all the bravado exited the stage, she found she enjoyed this woman's company far more than she'd ever thought.

They took slow, careful steps out of the ocean, Aubrey leading the way, and even when they passed the wet sand to meet the dry part, they didn't stop holding hands.

Selina was tempted to pull away, but somehow, she got the sense Aubrey needed the lifeline tonight, like Selina had needed the connection to wade into the water. The grains of sand stuck to her wet feet, coating them as they strolled along the length of the shore, the waves lapping endlessly into the distance. Several groups sat in flimsy chairs, camping on the beach, drinking, and celebrating, but they continued their solitary stroll under the moonlight.

"Hey, Selina?" Aubrey said, glancing her way. Their eyes met, and Selina needed to repress the shiver trickling through her veins. The raw vulnerability in that tone made her curious, a flutter of her pulse she didn't often experience. Aubrey swallowed, her neck bobbing. "Thank you."

Selina's lips turned up before she could help herself. "Don't know what you're thanking me for," she responded. "I'm just taking a nighttime stroll."

Aubrey shook her head, but a wry grin clung to her lips as she squeezed Selina's hand again.

The woman she'd encountered tonight was dangerous in a way she'd never been before.

Good thing the truce ended soon. They'd return to their bickering by tomorrow morning, and she could banish all thoughts of this vulnerable, real Aubrey Moore from her mind.

CHAPTER THREE

Aubrey woke up to the scent of bacon, cheese, and something else delicious cooking. One of the bonuses of renting a house with Sky Jenkins for a week was that her chef bestie made fucking next-level meals. Still, they ate out most of the time at the quirky restaurants scattered in the area. After all, the whole crew was on break from work here.

She thumped out of bed in a sports bra and a pair of running shorts. She should've been out there jogging at daybreak, but after last night, she'd let herself sleep in. She checked her phone. No updates from Chels, which could be a good or bad thing. Fuck. She'd have to tell everyone this morning.

Last night had been an escape she'd never expected. Whatever demon possessed her tongue to invite Selina Beckett on a walk to the beach had also pushed her into word vomiting her issues all over the woman she spent most of her time teasing. And yet, Selina's company had been the exact medicine she needed. The woman didn't dole out the sad puppy eyes that made her skin crawl or the pitying "ohs" at the mention of the big C. Instead, her honest, frank responses were a welcome dose of realism.

Except their truce had been one night only.

Aubs strode down the steps, following the scents to the kitchen. Sky stood behind the skillet, fast assembling toasted English muffins, eggs, bacon, and sharp cheddar into breakfast sandwiches that looked mouthwatering. Mia sat on the couch in the main room, a sketchbook out in front of her as she doodled. Kyle lounged in her running shorts and sweaty tank top, staring at the ceiling.

"And she arrives at last," Sky announced, glancing up to meet her eyes. An impish grin played on her lips. "How was your spin in the sheets with blondie last night? Usually you at least swing by before you vanish."

Aubs opened her mouth, not sure what might spill from her mouth. She should tell the others about the phone call from Chels, but everyone looked so cozy here. She didn't want to splatter wet paint all over the scene yet. Maybe later in the day. Maybe tonight she could tell them. The idea of dealing with the mopey sad eyes made her want to keep on avoiding the topic.

Kyle glanced at her. "Didn't see her walking home with blondie last night." Their gazes met.

Well damn, Kyle must've spotted her and Selina returning from the beach. They'd been out for a while, but she'd thought the others were still at the bar.

"Ah, yeah, blondie and I weren't meshing, so I chatted up someone else." Aubs didn't miss the pointed glance Kyle gave her with those sharp, all-seeing sparrow eyes. Of course, they'd be having a conversation later. Given a little time, Aubrey might be able to spin some believable bullshit. "You go for your run, Kyle?"

Kyle plucked the saturated shirt off of her chest. "I already went, Aubs. Not all of us had strenuous nights. I sent a chick running away from me in tears and gave the hell up after that stint of mortification."

A slight pang of disappointment thudded in Aubrey's chest. Last night set her off-kilter from the others, and this distance she didn't like had spread between them. Could probably bridge it easy enough, but that required opening her big mouth. Later. She'd bring up Mom's situation later.

"What did you say?" Aubs asked, curiosity getting the better of her.

"That her nail color looked like blood." Kyle heaved out a sigh, spearing fingers through her hair. "I meant it as a compliment."

Sky met eyes with Aubrey, and the both of them tried to hide their snorts. Kyle was a goddamn catch, but she needed to start as friends with a potential partner so the chick could understand Ky and her sense of humor. The bar approach had never been her forte, and yet Aubrey didn't know many other options. Not everyone had their high school best friends waiting in the wings to fall for them like Sky and Mia.

"All right, ladies, eat up," Sky said, plating the breakfast sandwiches and passing them over.

Aubrey's stomach rumbled as she snagged a plate, the scent of crisp bacon, salty cheese, and toasted English muffins making her salivate. She sat at one of the seats by the kitchen table and took a bite, relishing how all the deliciousness danced across her tongue.

Oh, fuck it. She needed to tell the girls.

"Okay, guys, I'm going to bring this up once, but

take all of your concern and shove it, because I'm still planning on enjoying this vacation." She could feel the stares bearing down on her, their gazes curious, but she didn't look up, romancing her sandwich instead. "Chels called last night because Mom passed out and got taken to the hospital. No, we don't know what the issue is. Also, no, she doesn't want visitors. I'm doing okay. I just wanted to let you all know now."

Aubrey stopped, and only silence echoed around her. Okay, maybe she'd overdone it.

Sky plunked beside her with her breakfast. "Glad to see nothing gets in the way of the conquest for you." Despite the sarcastic response, Aubs caught the gentle look in Sky's eyes.

"You know me," she said with a shrug of her shoulders as she took another hearty bite of her food.

Mia chewed on her lip, meeting Sky's gaze. Unlike Sky, who could skate triple axels on the superficial, Mia wanted to hug everyone around her all the time. Kyle took the seat across from Aubrey. She didn't say anything, but their eyes met in the wordless communication they'd perfected over the years. Kyle was the only one who'd known Aubrey during Mom's struggle with cancer. She was also the only one who knew her before she'd started finding a new bed to warm every night in a desperate need to escape, if just for a little bit.

Yeah, she'd killed the chill and cozy vibe here.

Aubs wolfed down her sandwich, trying to cram every last bit in her mouth. She needed to go for her morning run, now more than ever, if only to ditch the awkward tension. When she glanced up, Mia stared at her like she wanted to reach out.

"You keep giving me those puppy dog eyes and I'll assume you're flirting," Aubs warned.

Mia let out a sigh and shook her head. "Christ, I understand why you and Sky bonded so fast." She glanced at Sky. "Have any random facts you want to lob onto your unwilling victims, beautiful?"

"Space apparently smells like seared steak," Sky volunteered with a grin.

Aubs snorted and finished the last few bites of her sandwich, far before anyone else was even close. "That was delicious, Sky," she said through open-mouthed bites. "I'm going to go for my run now."

If they needed to get their kumbayas out, they could do so without her. Last night she'd allowed herself the time to sit with it, but today, she needed to move, move, move.

She darted out the door and put her feet to the pavement, purposefully going the opposite direction of Selina's rental next door. Maybe the gorgeous owner of Renegades lay out on the porch again reading her swoony romance book and maybe she didn't, but Aubrey hadn't figured out how to re-engage after their temporary truce had ended.

Her feet pounded the pavement. The sun beat on her shoulders as she began to find her rhythm in the run. The houses whizzed by her as she maintained speed, falling into the regularity of the motion, the way her calves flexed, and how her breath came in sharp intakes. Truth be told, in a single night she'd learned far too much about the mysterious owner of Renegades to be able to erase any of that information from her mind.

The way Selina darted back from the ocean like the water might bite her. The fact that she'd opened a bar just to find somewhere to settle down. How she'd given up a night of her vacation to keep Aubrey company even though they'd done nothing but bicker until now.

Right. Bickering. Annoying Selina. The status quo was safe, nothing like the prickling curiosity that swept through her after last night. Tonight they'd hit the bars, a club, anywhere, and she'd find some hottie to lose herself in, and order would be restored. Her legs pumped like pistons while she raced around the block, time dissipating as her body moved in the run.

She circled around block after block until she found herself running back down their road again, those familiar houses whirring by. Sweat soaked her chest, and her sports bra was glued to her skin. She slowed as she came closer and closer to the end of the block. Who knew how long she'd been out there running, but it'd been enough to feel the burn in her muscles that told her she'd gotten her workout in.

As Aubs slowed to a stroll, she came nearer to Selina's house. The temptation reared up in a big way to peek at the front porch and see if her favorite Wiccan sat out there reading again. Not like she needed to see Selina or anything. She just had to return to normal, which meant descending upon her like the harbinger of irritation.

Drops of sweat slithered down her forehead, trickling down her neck and her back in the process. She was a gross fucking mess, but folks usually saw her at her sweatiest. Part of working as a kickboxing instructor meant she needed to show her clients she was just as capable of what she asked them to do. Aubs lifted on tiptoes to peek at the wicker seats, but they were all empty. Her chest sank, and she chewed her lower lip.

Enough. She'd be able to annoy Selina some other time.

Her exaggerated breaths heaved as she cooled down from the run. The scorch in her veins felt good, exactly what she'd needed. She couldn't help one more glance as she passed by the front porch of Selina's rental.

She was rewarded with the sight of the woman lying sprawled out on a blanket reading a book, probably another romance. Aubrey bit back a laugh. Of course, that was how she'd stumble upon Selina. She learned new things about the woman left and right. Honestly, all she'd known before last night was that Selina was a practicing Wiccan, that she owned Renegades, and that the woman detested Aubrey.

Aubs stuck her fingers in her mouth to let out an ear-piercing whistle.

Selina glanced up from her book. For a moment, the woman's gaze was curious, the way it had been last night. Then her expression shifted, those coffee eyes cooling off.

"Catcalls are passé," Selina called back. She lay on her stomach, propped by her elbows as she held her book aloft. The angle showcased her sloping curves, including one magnificent ass. She might be short, but damn, the woman packed a punch in a small package. The deep purple sundress she wore exposed her mesmerizing hazel skin which glowed with a coppery hue under the morning sun. Her amethyst earrings glittered in the light, as did the purple glass pendant around her neck.

"You're assuming a whole lot, Beckett," Aubs called, strolling up to her. "I might've been placing a call for Lassie. There's someone stuck in a nearby well." She creaked up the steps with her approach, but Selina didn't budge from her spot. Fine, then. Aubrey sank to the ground beside her and perched on her elbows.

"I don't suppose it's a gorgeous woman stuck in the well you're trying to fish out?" Selina asked, even though her gaze still fluttered over the pages of her book.

Aubrey's lips widened, her teeth poking out of her grin. "Come on, what else motivates me? I've long since been considered a cat lady."

"Please spare me the grotesque pussy jokes," Selina responded, her voice withering. "I just ate breakfast."

This was the normalcy she'd been expecting.

The wry comment should've been a drop of relief in a pool of agitation, but instead it was a stirred stick in the pond, muddying the waters even more. Selina offered what she'd asked for, but that felt hollow compared to their walk on the beach last night, where a force more powerful than an uppercut had shifted things between them.

Aubrey leaned in, catching her scent of orange blossom and amber. Before Selina could react, Aubs plucked the book from her hands. She skimmed the words before her, ignoring Selina's murderous gaze.

Her grin widened. "Oh, you were at the sexy parts."

Selina flicked her in the shoulder. "Which I would've been enjoying if not for the rude interruption."

"Why read about it when you could be experiencing the real thing?" Aubs asked, her voice growing husky without her permission. She couldn't help the shiver that ran through her when her gaze met Selina's. The woman was beyond stunning.

Selina pursed her lips, delivering a pointed glare in her direction. "Because unlike you, I prefer more than grunting in the dark with a stranger. These books aren't one-night stands but slow, developed relationships, and after the crash and burns I've had, it's nice to dream that the real thing exists out there."

Aubs opened her mouth, the smart response dying on her lips. She passed the book to Selina and bumped shoulders with her. "Someone like you will absolutely find that," she found herself saying in complete seriousness. "Even if I never do" remained stuck on her tongue, unwilling to budge.

Selina's eyes widened for a moment, a flash of surprise there that returned to the same languid stare she often delivered with the steadiness of a cat. "Is Aubrey Moore saying something... not antagonistic? Color me shocked."

The gentle teasing snapped Aubs out of her mini panic. "Don't take it too much to heart," Aubs responded, the words coming too fast. "I just didn't want you out playing the field—the competition's fierce enough as is." Christ, that sounded half-assed, even to herself.

"Right," Selina said, her lips curling in a knowing smile.

Aubs pushed up from the front porch and smacked at her legs to brush away the granules of dirt that clung to them. "What are you and the ladies up to for the day?"

Selina crooked an eyebrow. "Why, planning on stalking me more?"

Aubrey shook her head. "You wish, sweetheart." She blew a kiss in Selina's direction and sauntered away. "I've got an entire sea of women to choose from down at the beach. No need to beg."

"Isn't that half the fun?" Selina murmured, challenge in her elegant arched brow.

Holy hell, this woman. Heat crawled up Aubrey's insides as she shook her head and began jogging the rest of the way back to the house. She needed to get out to the beaches and start flirting with women who didn't fuck with her head like Selina Beckett did.

Aubrey needed to staunch the curiosity brimming inside her before it spread.

CHAPTER FOUR

"Wait, you're joining us at the beach?" Cassidy stared at Selina, jaw agape.

"Calm your tits, Cass. I'm just changing up the reading environment a little bit," Selina said, already regretting the decision. She shifted her stance in her black bikini, turquoise towel slung over her shoulder. All she could smell was coconut from the suntan lotion she'd slathered on, but the extra effort would be worth finishing her book by the rolling tides.

Aubrey Moore had absolutely zero to do with the decision.

Steph and her boyfriend Zane emerged from their shared room, ready to roll. "You're kidding me," Steph said, pulling back her wild ginger mane into a ponytail. "We don't have to drag you out kicking and screaming?"

"I mean, if you all continue acting so shocked and appalled, then maybe." Selina tugged at the tote on her shoulder, ignoring the prickle of her skin at their scrutiny. She loathed crowds, but if she could find some space to carve out on her own, the swarm wouldn't be so bad. Maybe she needed to put herself out there a little more and start engaging the women she found attractive rather than keeping them at a distance. Better than letting Aubrey Moore infiltrate her thoughts, since the one-night-stand queen had no interest in hanging up the title.

"Let's get going then, before you change your mind," Cass teased, grabbing a floppy hat and her tote bag before she made her way to the door. Selina strode after her, ducking through the doorframe to set out into the seaside breezes and sunshine. Her heart pounded in anticipation of viewing the beach in the daytime after last night. She'd taken her first steps into the water in a long while then, but today she preferred to sit back and watch those waves lap to shore from afar.

Steph and Zane lingered behind them, still in the thrall of moony eyes and murmured conversations since they'd just made it official a few months ago.

Selina kept her gaze straight ahead as she trekked down the asphalt in flip-flops that barely saved her feet from the sizzling heat. She'd been friends with Steph ever since she moved to the area, and while she couldn't be happier for her, she also couldn't help the scorpion sting of jealousy that followed either. After the abysmal way her last relationship ended a year ago, she'd been avoiding the dating scene like the TELA virus.

Finding Katerina in *their* bed with another woman had just about broken her.

Selina sealed her lips. She wouldn't waste her mileage on frivolous dates until she was ready, and she wouldn't go after anyone who posted no strings attached on their Tinder profile. Whenever she tended bar at Renegades, she stacked up so many numbers that she could create her own phone book. She didn't bother calling them anymore. She'd learned her lesson.

The moment they hit Rehoboth Beach, her nose wrinkled in distaste. The sheer amount of people was nauseating. The sea was barely visible at all. Not like last night when the immense mass spanned out before them with few folks crowding the beach. The shore at night contained a tinge of melancholy, but walking along it with Aubrey had made it memorable, like they'd been isolated from the chaos.

Cass swept past her, tote bag brushing against Selina's arm. "I see some folks we know. Let's see if they'll let us steal some space."

"How do people find this enjoyable, again?" Selina asked, wishing she'd stayed back at the rental. She could easily spend a week basking in the sea breezes, soaking in the sunshine, and blowing through book after book by her lonesome.

Steph flicked her in the side, detaching from Zane for a moment. "Because it's the warmest part of the day, which makes it the best time to dip into the ocean."

"Which means little when you want to bask and read," Selina commented dryly as she hid a shudder. None of her friends knew about her phobia because she didn't prefer to shout it to the streets. Cass led them past a sea of red and blue coolers, multicolored towels, beach umbrellas, and screaming children who'd gotten sand in their eyes. About midway through the crowd, Cass began to wave. Selina adjusted her sunglasses on the bridge of her nose, trying to follow Cass's gaze to see who they headed toward.

Not like she could spot much of anything with

the mess of people far taller than her blocking the way. Hell, even some of the umbrellas had her beat.

"Hey, guys," Cass called out. "Mind if we steal some space?"

"Come join us," a voice sounded in return, familiar and low. Selina glanced up to see Sky Jenkins standing there in board shorts and a tank top, her arm curled around her girlfriend Mia's waist. Selina's stomach sank. Of course, if Sky and Mia were here, that meant....

Her gaze skated around the area, but she didn't spot Aubrey, just their friend Kyle splayed out on a towel in a navy-blue one-piece. Selina didn't know if she should be relieved or disappointed. Chances were Aubrey was wandering through the crowds of women, flashing a smile, crooking a finger, and leading them back to her rental.

Selina brought her towel out and settled next to Kyle. "You seem to have the right idea here."

Kyle glanced up at her. "Feel free to join me," she said. "I'm not one for bodysurfing, picking up women, or any of the things Aubs seems to be hurling herself into right now."

Selina pointedly ignored the mention of Aubrey's name as she settled onto the towel beside

Kyle, lying on her stomach. She'd tucked her Kindle into the small tote she'd dragged at her side.

"I'm not into any of those things either," Selina said, enjoying how Kyle ducked her head. The woman seemed sweet—far too sweet for someone like her, but exactly the sort of person who didn't ruffle her feathers. Unlike the womanizer they both knew.

"Yeah, but you at least have game with the ladies." Kyle scrubbed her hair. "I've seen you flash flirty grins at Renegades before. My attempt at a seductive smile makes it look like I'm having a stroke."

Selina snorted and placed her Kindle on the towel in front of her. "Here, why don't you try practicing with me? I can give you an honest appraisal, free of charge."

Kyle's eyes creased, and her lips turned up in an adorable grin. "Thanks, though I'm already feeling embarrassed."

"That," Selina said, pointing to Kyle's face. "Girlie, I can pull off seductive because I've got a permanent case of RBF. When you're trying to woo other women, you've got to lead with yourself and what's natural. And for you? That sweet, shy smile will draw the women in throngs."

Kyle's cheeks lit up in a furious blush, and she buried her face into the towel in front of her. "Thank you, Selina."

Her lips quirked. If only she felt those stirrings for someone gentle and cute like this. Kyle didn't seem the sort to juggle with hearts and break them. She glanced toward the ocean in front of them, the foamy crests glittering as they crashed onto the shore. A figure swam further out, and as one of the big waves swelled, they rode along with the crest. A moment later they washed up on the shore, and Selina realized who it was.

Of course Aubrey would be out hurling herself into waves, like the monstrous things wouldn't drag her out to the deep. The woman seemed to live for danger and excitement, for diving into the next momentary thrill. She was the exact sort of trouble Selina needed to avoid. When Aubrey rose to her feet, the sun gleamed over her tanned skin, causing it to glow bronze. Strands of her wet ponytail were plastered on her shoulders and the side of her neck. The high-neck black bikini she wore revealed those strong, corded thighs, muscular arms, and defined, bitable abs.

Aubrey's gaze swung in their direction, and Selina's heart stuttered. Fuck.

So, Aubrey was gorgeous. Selina knew that and had still managed to avoid her advances for years. She needed to bury herself in a book and look away from the charming woman fast approaching them. Based on the glint in her eyes, Aubrey would be heading her way to irritate her as usual. Selina loved and loathed the attention, mostly because that same attention would swing elsewhere the moment an easy lay threw herself tits-first at Aubrey.

She popped open her Kindle and stared at the words on the screen, none of them registering. In her peripheral, she could see Aubrey's slow approach. She walked with smooth, liquid strides up the shore as she headed toward them.

"What are you reading?" Kyle's voice sliced through her thoughts, a welcome distraction. Behind them, Cass lounged in the small beach chair she'd brought, sitting alongside Mia and Sky, who climbed all over each other. Zane and Steph had already headed toward the ocean for a dip.

"A cute romance about dueling bakers in the same town," Selina volunteered. No one expected her to read romance—at least based on the skeptical expressions she received every time she mentioned her book preferences, but she loved the depth of the emotions and the warmth that emanated off the pages, sinking into all the lonely cracks in her life.

Kyle grinned. "That sounds like a blast. I'm regretting not bringing a book, though chances are I won't last much longer. I burn too fast to do the whole-day beach thing like the rest of these ladies."

"I may sneak off too," Selina murmured, trying to ignore the fast-approaching presence who radiated like a nuclear reactor. "I might enjoy basking in the sun for a bit, but I'm not huge on all these crowds."

Kyle's nose wrinkled, emphasizing her freckles. "I bet you're not loving the main sprawl of town then."

Selina shrugged. "I enjoy quieter places. They exist around here, but you have to look around a little to find them."

A shadow stretched over them, and a moment later, Aubrey descended into the space between them, sending grains of sand flying all over their towels.

Selina shot her a look. "Graceful."

Aubrey offered a toothy grin, sand coating her wet arms, legs, and torso. "What are the two of you chatting about? I don't suppose Selina's trying to fill you with hateful propaganda toward me, Ky?"

"Like she could tell me anything I don't already

know." Kyle shook her head, a rueful smile on her lips. "Selina's been a complete sweetheart."

Aubrey's brows drew together in mock surprise. "You? Being a sweetheart? Is this a cry for help? Have you been body snatched?"

"What can I say? You justify my resting bitch face every time, Aubrey Moore," Selina drawled.

Aubrey rolled onto her back, more sand sticking to the wet areas on her skin. She pretended to stab herself in the chest, a motion Selina couldn't help but follow with the way her chest heaved and those tight abs contracted. "Cruel barbs."

"Not if they're true," Selina responded, her heart pumping a little harder. Swapping snark with Aubrey had become a professional sport for them both—apart from last night and the odd moment earlier. Aubrey's earnest words lingered, percolating around her brain in a dangerous swirl.

Kyle watched them, curiosity in those dark eyes, a knowing look Selina didn't trust. The woman seemed to be even more of an observer than her best friend, and she didn't want those telepathic probes coming anywhere near her traitorous thoughts.

Aubrey rolled onto her stomach in a constant flurry of motion, as if she couldn't stop moving. From the moment they'd met, Aubrey had always been in motion, whether going on runs, sweeping in to chat up women at the bar, running drills in the kickboxing studio, or firing off words a mile a minute. Selina didn't know how anyone could keep up.

"I'm going to head back to the rental," Kyle said, poking at her arm. "I'm starting to get pink. Want my towel, Aubs?"

"Is that a hint I need to dry off?" Aubrey asked, a glint in her eyes as she looked up.

"Either that, or I don't want to carry home the towel you covered in wet sand," Kyle said with a grin. Her gaze skated over the both of them, and Selina's heart beat a little harder. Clever, clever woman.

Kyle offered a wave. "Great seeing you, Selina. Hopefully, we'll catch you at the bars later. I think we're heading to Dante's Nightclub."

"You guys should join us," Sky called out from behind. "You're staying at the rental near ours, right?"

"Sounds better than the nonexistent plans I had for tonight," Cass chimed in.

Selina heaved out an internal sigh. Avoiding Aubrey Moore just became even harder.

Aubrey settled down on Kyle's towel, even though her elbow still rested precariously close to

Selina's. "Does that mean I get to witness Selina Beckett tear up the dance floor tonight?"

"You're making wild assumptions that I'd show to a nightclub," Selina responded, her tone dry, as if she might stand a chance at hiding how her heart beat at Aubrey's proximity.

"You don't need to be embarrassed if you can't dance," Aubrey teased, her wicked eyes glinting. "Maybe you just need the right teacher."

Cass snorted from behind them. "Oh honey, you don't even know how wrong you are. Our dear Miss Beckett used to swing her hips as a backup dancer to different artists on tour. She'd school you so bad you'd be trying to return to yesterday."

Selina bit back a groan. Of course Cass would bring up those couple of years before she moved to Wilmington and opened her own bar. She stuck up her middle finger in response. Selina loved to dance, but she hated people knowing her business. She especially hated Aubrey Moore knowing her business.

Aubrey's jaw dropped, and she poked her in the shoulder. "No fucking way. Are there videos?"

Selina flexed her jaw, willing Cass with her mind to shut her damn mouth.

"I'm pretty sure if I say any more, I'm asking to

get buried in the sand," Cass called back, amusement in her tone.

"You have to show me them," Aubrey demanded, jabbing her in the shoulder again with that insistent poker finger. "Or, better yet, show up tonight and whip out some of those moves."

"How about no to both?" Selina responded. Even as she said the words, her gut stirred with the urge to head out to the dance floor and lose herself in the music for a little while. The idea of Aubrey's eyes glued to her didn't influence the decision at all.

"Ignore Aubs," Mia called over. "We'd love for you to join us, and there's no pressure to dance."

"You can dance if you want to," Aubs started, and Sky let out an immediate groan. "You can leave your friends behind...."

Selina arched an eyebrow. "You can 'Safety Dance' all you like, sunshine, but me dancing is going to remain a figment of your imagination."

"My imagination's particularly filthy," Aubrey shot back.

"Speaking of, don't you have a dozen women to go hit on?" Selina responded in a feeble attempt to push Aubrey's focus in any other direction. The longer Aubrey maintained eye contact, the harder it became to ignore her body's response. Her imagination went rampant at the idea of dirty dancing with the woman mere inches from her. A flush crawled through her body, but she dismissed it as overheating from the intense sun.

Aubrey shrugged and offered another grin. "Why leave when I'm having so much fun here?" She fluttered her eyelashes, and Selina's heart did another flip in her chest.

Oh, she was so fucked.

To make matters worse, she would probably go to the damn club with them tonight.

CHAPTER FIVE

Any normal night of heading to Dante's Nightclub, or really, any club, and Aubrey would be ready to prowl. This was her longest dry spell on any trip to Rehoboth Beach. She'd already been here for a few days and hadn't had a single woman in her bed.

However, when she got home from the beach and checked her texts, the one from Chels just stated that Mom needed to stay at the hospital for more testing. Never a good sign, not with a cancer survivor. Aubrey should be throwing herself into the nearest distraction, but she couldn't quite shake the other night with Selina. The comfort she'd found from simply walking on the beach in silence had been more than she'd felt in a long, long while.

"I feel like I need to starfish around you to keep

other women away," Sky murmured into Mia's ear as they walked along. While Sky dressed in loose black pants and a tight white tank top, Mia went for femme with her low-cut lilac dress that unfurled around mid-thigh. Sky clutched her by the waist in a fit of possession. Aubrey's lips quirked. A year ago, her friend had been just as bad as Aubrey when it came to letting people in. She was glad to see the change, even if it made her jealous as shit.

"Just fling them my way," Kyle said. "Not toward Aubs." She adjusted the short shirt that exposed her belly button. A pair of army-green shorts accented the look. Kyle always managed to look adorable, and if she'd ever have faith in her own attractiveness, she might be able to snag herself a date. Instead, she retreated at the first sign of trouble over and over again. "We know who she's got locked and loaded in her sights tonight."

"You mean any fox who happens to wander my way?" Aubs said, not missing a beat. Even still, she caught the curiosity in Kyle's eyes. Her bestie saw far too much. She brushed her palms down on the little black dress she donned for tonight, a slim, practical cut that exposed plenty of thigh.

"Like we haven't seen the way you've been eye-fucking Selina," Sky commented from behind.

Aubrey resisted the urge to strangle her. "You and I both know tormenting Selina's a pastime of mine. She just made it more convenient by renting the house next to ours."

Ky lifted an eyebrow. "If you genuinely feel something for her, you know we'd never give you shit, Aubs. She's pretty fantastic, and I've never met anyone who could keep up with your ego like she does."

A flush rolled through Aubrey, followed by ice. Feeling anything for the women she slept with, the ones she chased, had been forbidden for so, so long. She'd locked that door tight the moment she got the pronouncement about Mom's cancer and her girlfriend, Lila, bailed, because supporting her through that was too hard.

No one chose difficult, and she'd never be anything but.

"You're assuming Selina won't murder her within five minutes. Have you ever seen them interact at Renegades?" Sky responded from behind.

Aubs forced a grin. "I'm certain if looks could poison, I would've died years ago. Selina's hot—no one's denying that—but you know me. I'd get bored with no variety, and that girl's all about settling down." She faked a shudder, though based on the way Kyle's contemplative hazel eyes fixated on her, the woman didn't believe her in the slightest.

Dante's Nightclub stood out at the end of the boardwalk with white awnings and a large red neon sign. The dark pulse of music beckoned them forward. Aubrey already couldn't wait to get out on the dance floor and move, to pack these conflicting feelings away for a while. Some of the red lights from inside poured out from the entrance, like the women were being beckoned into the inferno. A few folks crowded out around the front, chatting amid clouds of cigarette smoke. Aubs couldn't help how her gaze lingered on each person as if she might spot Selina among them.

The woman had promised to show off her dance moves. That was all.

Then Aubs would return to her busy schedule of chatting up women at the bar and bringing them back to her bed to enjoy each other until the late hours.

After that, she'd kick them out and spend the rest of the night glancing between her phone and the ceiling, as if answers might arrive at any point. The pulse of worry deafened more than the ocean, and at night, there was no escaping it. Great plan on her part.

"Ready to go strut your stuff, Ky?" Aubs asked, elbowing her in the side.

"As long as we're far enough away from Mia and Sky's massive displays of PDA," Ky mock whispered to her.

Mia grinned and planted another kiss on Sky's lips, making it drawn out and sloppy. "We aim to please."

Aubs felt the little tug in her gut again, the sear of jealousy that Sky had gotten out of their miserable circle of three—she'd scored the real deal in the love department. Next would be Ky, because Ky deserved to find the happiness she'd been searching for, and then Aubrey'd be by her lonesome, still hitting up the bars and the clubs for a new woman to take home with her.

"I need a goddamn drink," Aubs muttered, grabbing for the door to the club and yanking it open. The scent of sweat, sunscreen, and warring colognes greeted her at once. Bars lined the sides of the place, as well as a few stools spaced around the center of the club. In the back, a dance floor spread across the space, flashing red lights pulsing onto the black floors. A steady stream of people filtered inside and out through the side entrance that led onto the deck strung with bulb lights where another speaker pulsed music out for the patrons.

She marched to the bar, not waiting for everyone else. Some doe-eyed honey swung her way, the black tank top she wore showcasing lithe arm muscles.

"What can I get for you, babe?"

Aubs's tongue trailed over her lips. Normally, this would be her chance to dive in with a line to reel her in. But the situation at home pulsed in the back of her brain, louder than the music, and she needed something stronger to shut those worries out. "Long Island iced tea," she responded, drumming her fingertips on the counter.

The bartender tossed her a flirty wink and sashayed over to the glasses to get started. Ky slid up beside her.

"Okay, baby doll, it's lesson time," Aubrey responded, nudging Ky in the side. "Try to flirt when you order your drink."

Ky shot her a glare, blowing strands of her hair out of her face. "You say that like flirting's so easy."

"You're a fucking catch, and the world should know it," Aubrey responded, an itch crawling up her legs to get out on the dance floor and move. The music bumped tonight, a heavy thump, thump, thump that reverberated through her bones.

Flirty Bartender swung back over with the Long Island iced tea and placed it in front of Aubs. She passed the cash over and offered a grin in response. Any normal night, she'd be leaning across the counter, exposing an ample view of her tits and trying to chat up this woman, but she couldn't sit still for anything. Aubrey's gaze darted to the napkin beneath the drink, catching the scrawled numbers.

"And what can I get for you?" The bartender swung her attention to Kyle, though not without one last lingering look in Aubrey's direction.

Ky sucked in a deep breath for a moment and looked at the bartender. "Gin and tonic, please." When the woman offered a nod, Kyle responded with one of her gorgeous grins, the real ones she melted into so often. The bartender's lip quirked up in response as she sauntered away to get the drink started.

"Where the hell did that come from?" Aubrey nudged her in the side. "Damn, heartbreaker."

Ky shot her a pointed look. "I'm following Selina's advice instead of yours."

Aubs ran the tip of her tongue along her teeth. Damn the woman and the way she crept into every thought and conversation as of late. Ky's gaze shifted past her, and she lifted her hand to wave.

Aubrey turned around to spot the crew from earlier approaching. She could barely remember the names of Selina's friends, but that didn't matter when her gaze landed on the woman herself.

The red lights glided over all the bare skin—and a lot of it. Selina wore a slinky black dress, the scoop neck perilously low and the black skirt hiked up at the sides, exposing plenty of thigh. God, the woman had thighs Aubrey wanted to memorize, and with the chunky silver jewelry Selina wore, her eyeliner thick and smoky, and her lips the color of a Red Delicious, Aubrey found herself spellbound.

"You're drooling," Ky said, leaning in close enough so her words didn't carry.

Aubrey drew her mouth closed again. Right. Mortal enemies. Ignore the way her core was pulsing at the sight of this woman decked out like a fucking sex dream under these throbbing red lights. She took a sip of her drink, forcing her gaze away from the gorgeous woman who glided toward them. And if Selina danced? Watching her move in that slinky dress might kill her. The scorch of sugary alcohol lingered on her tongue, even if the drink didn't distract her nearly as much as she'd hoped.

"I don't know what you're talking about," Aubrey

responded in a lofty tone, delivering Ky a pointed glance.

Kyle snorted. "You trying to be intimidating doesn't work. And you can dodge around it all you like—I'm just saying, the attraction's screamingly obvious. Having said that, I'm going to dive onto the dance floor."

Aubrey flicked her in the side. She loved-hated Ky right now.

"Hey guys," Cass said, striding toward them. "You already grab drinks? Where are Sky and Mia?"

"Out on the floor, slobbering all over each other like the disgusting couple they are," Aubrey responded.

"I think they're sweet," Selina challenged, a subtle flare in her eyes.

"What would be sweet is to see those dance moves you bragged about earlier," Aubrey responded, leaning with her back against the bar, elbows digging into the counter.

Selina's gaze drifted to the napkin under her drink and sharpened there. Aubrey resisted the urge to hide the scrawled number or to toss the napkin in the trash since the bartender had slunk up to get the newcomers some beverages.

"Getting started early?" Selina asked, stepping to

the counter beside Aubrey. "And if I recall, there was no bragging involved on my part, just a firm reminder that you're never going to see me dance."

Selina ordered a pint of porter and flashed the bartender the sort of dazzling grin that never got aimed Aubrey's way. Most of the time she received grimaces or eye rolls from the owner of Renegades.

"I think that sounds like a challenge to me," Aubs said, sidling a little closer to Selina.

Selina arched a single curved brow. "Everything sounds like a challenge to you."

"If you're not here to dance, then what do you plan on doing?" Aubs asked, taking another sip from her drink. The headiness of the booze began to sink into her veins, making her whole body feel a little warmer.

"People watching," Selina responded, her lips pursed as she scanned out over the crowd. "Once you've flung yourself at your latest conquest, I'll be free to hit the dance floor."

"Not fucking fair, Selina Beckett," Aubrey responded, a slight grin slipping across her lips. "You know how much I want to see those moves you're hiding."

Selina glanced her way, and for a moment, she

caught something real flickering in her dark gaze. A question?

Or, a dare. As in how badly did she want to see Selina dance?

More than she wanted to strip the bar owner down and devour her pussy. The idea of watching Selina's hips move captivated her like nothing else. She chewed on her bottom lip at the idea of this gorgeous woman moving on the dance floor with that hypnotizing grace at her command. Fuck, Aubrey'd pass out.

Aubrey met her gaze, eyes heating. "Fine, then I don't want to hear you complaining when I hang around you all damn night."

"Whatever will the women of Rehoboth do?" Selina said, tossing a hand over her forehead even as the sarcasm dripped from her lips.

The bartender plunked the beer next to Selina, scanning back and forth between the two of them. The woman bobbed her head and mouthed, "Good luck."

Goddamn, was she that transparent?

"The women of Rehoboth can survive tonight," Aubrey said, plastering a smile on her face. She didn't know where the hell she was going with any of this, but ever since she'd realized how calming Selina's presence was, she craved more. She'd probably regret this tomorrow, or even a day after, but part of her wanted to plunge into the water and leave those fears behind. "Tonight, I'm going to stick by your side until you dance for me."

Selina's brows lifted, but she masked her surprise with her trademark wan smile. "You'll be waiting a long time, sunshine."

———

CHAPTER SIX

THREE BEERS IN, AND SELINA HAD BEGUN TO realize Aubrey was serious.

After arriving to find the woman up to her usual tricks, number scrawled on a napkin and all, any tendrils of hope that had begun to unfurl were snuffed out. However, when Aubrey sat and people watched with her for hours, swapping jabs back and forth and trying to tempt her out on the dance floor, something shifted. Aubrey had long ago tossed the napkin with the number into the trash, and she lingered close enough that their elbows and thighs kept bumping into each other. The fresh scent of sage and lemon coming from the woman dizzied Selina's mind.

Selina lifted her wrist as if she was checking her

nonexistent watch. "You're running out of hours to bring someone home."

Aubrey shrugged and sipped on her rum and coke, the second drink of the night. "There's no law that says I have to drag a woman home with me nightly. You make it sound like I'm the sex addict version of Jack the Ripper."

Selina's lips quirked in amusement. "If the shoe fits."

"You take that back," Aubrey said, lobbing a light punch at her arm. "I'm waiting for you to take to the dance floor. I'm told I can be quite persistent."

"Persistent is one word for it. Others include obnoxious, stubborn... need I keep going?" An open grin broke out on her face this time, the sort she usually restrained around Aubrey Moore.

Aubrey's jaw dropped, and she stared at her like she'd descended from an alien planet.

Self-consciousness flushed through Selina. "What, did I get something on my face? Lipstick smear?"

"So that's what a real smile from you looks like?" Aubrey said, a little breathless. "I knew you were beautiful, but... *damn.*"

Selina's cheeks heated in response. When Aubrey threw out slick lines, she had no problem evading them, but the genuine surprise she expressed? Words dried on her tongue, and Selina wasn't sure what to say next. Her heart wanted to leap out of her chest at the wonder on Aubrey's face when she looked at Selina, and how those chestnut eyes peered right into her tonight. The more Selina had begun to see of the real woman beyond the cockiness and swagger, the more she'd found herself ensnared.

"Finish your drink, Moore," Selina said, her voice a bit gruff as she made the desperate attempt to distract. "Let's head out to the dance floor."

Aubrey's eyes lit up. "I thought you were never going to dance in front of me," she teased before taking a big gulp of her rum and coke.

"What's to say I'm not going to just stand there and watch you?" Selina responded, cocking an eyebrow. She clung to their back-and-forth like a lifeline right now. She had every ounce of resistance in her arsenal for the womanizer who took a different girl home every night but none for this woman who dropped earnest compliments like grenades.

"I'd be fine with your eyes on me," Aubrey responded, her voice husky and her gaze heated.

Selina's mind spun as desire kicked her square in the chest. This version of Aubrey ignited an attraction she hadn't experienced in years, the incendiary, throat-squeezing, heart-pounding type she only read about in books. Which was dangerous because Aubrey Moore could shatter her heart in a thousand pieces with no remorse, but Selina couldn't seem to help herself while they were down here in Rehoboth, the ocean and summer breezes casting a spell over her.

One week. They were going to be here for one week before circumstances returned to normal, and they headed back to Wilmington where she had to watch Aubrey plow through the women in her bar. She could hold out one week without crossing too far over the line.

Aubrey placed the empty glass onto the bar counter and tilted her head toward the dance floor. "Promises were made. Let's head out."

The closer they got to the back, the more the red beams glowed brighter, flashing with the throb-throb-throb of the music. The throngs of people grew more difficult to navigate around, so when Aubrey reached back to grab her hand, Selina went with it. Together, they dodged past a sea of elbows and swinging hips, the stench of sweat, Black Orchid, and Eau de Chanel wafting through the people around them.

Aubrey led them over to the fringes of the crowd

with enough space to move so they wouldn't be flush against every other body dominating the dance floor. A massive fan blew breezes onto the dancers, and the cooling gust sent a shiver racing up Selina's spine. Once they stepped onto the lacquered tiles, her body felt the beat of the music as it traveled through her, begging to extend out through her arms and legs.

Despite the sudden urge to dance, part of her didn't want to. Once she swung her hips for a little bit and Aubrey realized she wasn't about to hop into bed with her, the woman would get bored. Then she'd be off, chasing after the next lonely blonde by the bar. As much as Selina hated to admit it, she'd enjoyed Aubrey's company this week.

Aubrey leaned in, her lips brushing against her ear. The sensation made her shiver. "If you're too embarrassed, I can start dancing first," Aubrey taunted.

Selina shot her a pointed look but didn't dignify her dig with a response. Instead, she sucked in a deep steadying breath and let the music flow through her. Dancing came as second nature, something she did while cleaning at home, at the club, or even behind the bar on slower nights when a song she loved came on.

Selina swung her hips in time to the beat, and

from there, the rest of her body followed. She closed her eyes for a moment, feeling out the song, the rhythm, the way her body's expression wanted to unfold, and all of her training snapped into place. The bass picked up, and she sank into the melody, beginning to twist and writhe to the music with every movement under her control. She swayed back and forth in time, her foot tapping out the beat as she followed the flow.

Selina's eyes snapped back open even though she didn't stop moving, her arms weaving up as her hips twisted down. The red lights cascaded over her to the beat of the music, and she glanced over at Aubrey, who stood there unmoving beside her. The woman studied her with the sort of focus reserved for works of art in galleries, and her entire body flushed, her skin feeling tighter under the intense gaze.

Truth be told, she didn't hate having Aubrey's sole attention.

Truth be told, she'd been curious about what that would be like ever since Aubrey started showing up at Renegades and charming women out of their seats and into her bed.

Truth be told, the curious desire that welled inside her was addictive, which meant this path was destined for a wreck.

"Don't tell me you're going to leave me dancing alone," Selina said, stretching a hand out in invitation.

Aubrey slid her palm across hers, and Selina took control. In a few fluid movements, she brought Aubrey flush against her as she continued to dance to the music, the undulating flow something she'd love to lose herself in. This close, heat sizzled between their bodies, the red lights flashing over Aubrey's corded thighs exposed in her short black dress, which was sporty, like everything she wore.

"Damn, woman," Aubrey murmured in her ear. "Cass wasn't exaggerating. You know how to *move*." The hushed tone in her voice, like she'd stumbled upon a revelation, sent a shiver up Selina's spine.

"I'm not prone to extravagant lies," Selina responded, stepping away and then drawing them flush again. Aubrey moved in time with her, following direction better than expected. "Unlike someone we both know."

Aubrey's lips quirked. A sheen of sweat glistened on her shoulders and the slope of her neck, and the desire to lean in and lick a droplet off rose in Selina something fierce. They danced an inch apart, breath puffing between them and the tension crackling like a campfire. When Aubrey's gaze rose to meet hers, the breath snagged in Selina's throat. She dated women she'd been head over heels for, but she didn't think anyone had ever looked at her like *that*.

Aubrey stared at her like she had on the first night. They'd gazed out to the horizon to where the scorched sky met with the blackened waves that were consuming, all-encompassing.

Selina took the next rise and fall in the music to twirl herself around, breaking their gaze before she combusted. Even with her back to Aubrey, she could feel the woman's presence an inch from her, swaying along with the music. Selina continued driving her hips side to side, swinging them around in time with the song. A second later, Aubrey's hands settled on her hips, tentatively resting as if asking for permission.

Oh, holy hell. If the space between them had been intense, it couldn't compare to this woman's touch. Selina thrust her ass back to the heavy bass line of the music, and Aubrey's hands settled firmer on her hips, her palms imprinting through the flimsy fabric of her dress like brands. Selina's underwear was soaked, but at least that she could hide. Not like she could admit how turned on this woman made her.

Her heart thumped to the same dark beat as the

music as she twisted and turned, grinding against Aubrey like she wasn't dropping paper into open flame. The woman swayed behind her, the steady pressure of her palms causing Selina's pussy to ignite. She rarely indulged in this closeness with anyone outside of a relationship.

Her ass brushed back against Aubrey again, and the woman let out a low, almost indecipherable moan. The sound shot a burst of lust through Selina's veins. If this went any further, she'd be dragging Aubrey to the bathroom, damn the consequences, and begging the woman to fuck her until she forgot her principles. All she could think of was the steadying hands on her hips, the jolt of skin-to-skin contact when their bodies brushed together, and Aubrey's maddening scent mingling with sweat.

She needed to pull away before she lost her mind.

The song came to an end, and Selina took the chance to step away from Aubrey, breaking the connection between them. Honestly, she could've done that all night, but not without those sensations going to her head and pushing her to make decisions she'd regret. Just because Aubrey offered a few genuine moments didn't mean the woman suddenly wanted to update her relationship status. And Selina didn't want to waste time on hollow one-night stands or flings that whizzed by like the stop on a train.

Selina wiped her arm across her sticky forehead. She leaned in closer to Aubrey. "I'm going to catch some air and a smoke."

The unsaid lingered there. Aubrey had gotten what she'd been waiting for—the chance to see Selina dance, and it wasn't going any further. Selina sucked in a sharp breath of the heavy air, bracing herself for the woman's inevitable exit.

Aubrey crossed her arms over her chest. "Is this your weak-willed attempt to ditch me, Beckett? Like you'd be so lucky."

Selina's heart thumped a little harder. "If you want some smoke-filled fresh air, you're welcome to join."

"Well, when you put it like that, who could resist?" Aubrey responded, a charming grin on her lips. Selina's head spun, not from the dancing or the heat, but from the sheer proximity of this contradicting, confusing woman. She shook her head and began to weave her way around the crowd. This time, she reached back to grab Aubrey's hand, their palms pressing together.

She carved through the crowd, popping out by the door where the fresh air and steady stream of newcomers continued to enter in. Selina's heart beat harder than ever and not just from exertion. The feel of Aubrey's palm pressed against hers was heady, reminding her of their initial night here and the way they'd held hands and walked along the shore.

She slipped out through the door to find an open spot against the wall to lean. A moment later she snagged the cigarette pack and lighter from the inside of her boot, and Aubrey settled beside her.

"Where did your friends go?" Selina asked as she lit the end of her cigarette and sucked in the first steadying drag. As if the nicotine stood a chance at calming the mambo her nerves danced.

"Where did yours?" Aubrey asked back, a grin playing on her lips. Their eyes met, an electric current buzzing between them. They both knew they'd spent the entire night together, losing track of their friends the moment they connected. Aubrey wasn't admitting it out loud, and there was no way Selina would—not when she was trying to hold onto the threads of her common sense before they snapped.

"Touché," Selina said. She flicked ash on the ground before bringing the cigarette to her lips again. Aubrey's stare bored into her, lingering on her mouth in a way that coursed right down to her core. Selina knew sex would be on the table if she asked, but honestly, one-night stands didn't make her clock tick. She needed connection and security, and the older she got, the harder those things were to come by.

Aubrey's eyes lingered on her, and when Selina looked up, their gazes met. The slight sheen of vulnerability in Aubrey's had been there ever since the other night when she'd gotten the phone call from her sister.

"Any word on...." Selina let things trail off as she took in another drag of her cigarette.

"Nada," Aubrey responded, tapping the back of her head against the wall as she stared at the sky.

"Well, that's a shit situation," Selina responded. "Sure you don't want a drag?"

Aubrey's eyes lingered on her lips again, but she shook her head. "Sorry, sweetheart. My line of work requires healthy lungs." Her mouth shut for a moment and then she opened it again. "Thanks for asking without making a big deal. The wait's been agonizing, but spending all this time with my arch-nemesis has taken the edge off a lot."

Selina arched a brow. "Glad to be of service. I can deliver some extra barbs if masochism's what you need."

Aubrey flipped her the middle finger, a goofy

smile taking over her face. That look there was more dangerous than all the charm the woman levied. In these quiet moments, Selina'd somehow gotten to know Aubrey Moore better than most, and she couldn't turn the clock back and forget that side of her.

"Some company wouldn't be the worst," Aubrey commented, giving her a sidelong glance. "You're pretty damn distracting, Selina Beckett."

Her lips curled into a grin. "I aim to please."

Far too fast, the jabs and the disdain had softened between them. Even if nothing came out of this, even if she needed to wall herself away from Aubrey Moore for months afterward, she'd enjoy this truce while it lasted.

CHAPTER SEVEN

Aubrey woke early and went for her morning jog. To her disappointment, she didn't spot Selina out on the porch, probably because she wasn't a lunatic who woke up at six in the morning on vacation.

By the time she returned, showered, and headed down for breakfast, the house was still cemetery quiet. She wandered through the hallway and noticed Kyle's bedroom door was open. Well, damn, the woman must not have come home last night. She shot a text to Ky with a winky face and a thumbs up. It was about time Kyle indulged in a fling after all the years she spent feeling like a reject. Aubs wandered toward the room Mia and Sky shared, but before she lifted her fist to knock, she heard the telltale moan of morning sex.

In a rare twist of irony, it looked like everyone was getting laid but her. She'd come home last night and spent some quality time with her dildo, needing to burn off some of the tension that built up every time she was around Selina. The explosive orgasm that followed was part buildup and part imagining those lush lips locked with hers and Selina's fingers pumping inside her with all that coiled grace and control.

Aubrey knew Selina wasn't like her—she didn't sleep around, didn't do the one-night stand thing, and the moment Aubrey made the suggestion this fragile thing between them would shatter.

Yet for the first time in a long while, she didn't regret a thing. Certainly not the time she'd spent with Selina last night sitting and talking in front of the nightclub, then dancing close when they went back in. She hadn't gotten to know anyone that intimately in years. Not since Mom first got diagnosed.

Aubrey strode downstairs, her stomach rumbling. She needed food and coffee, but she didn't feel like cooking this morning. Still no word from Chels either, which could be good or bad.

She took a seat at one of the stools at the breakfast nook and whipped out her phone. Aubrey managed to get one phone number last night—the only one she wanted.

You up?

She tapped her foot on the base of the stool as she waited for a response. If she didn't hear anything, she'd roam on her own. A second later, her phone buzzed.

When I gave you my number, it was for contacting me at reasonable hours.

A wide grin spread on Aubrey's face before she could help herself. Selina always had snark to deliver, morning, noon, or night.

Want to grab coffee at the Silver Mug? I'm starving and under-caffeinated and might die.

The response came back immediately.

Drama queen. Give me five minutes.

Aubrey's heart sped up. Damnit. Selina wasn't the type to fuck around, and Aubrey wasn't the type to commit, but with Mom's hospital stay weighing over her, Aubrey couldn't help but fall for any comfort she could find. Once upon a time, she'd adored the distraction, the way those hookups quieted her racing mind, but recently, all they did was stir her thoughts into a frenzy.

Just coffee. They were getting coffee—that was

it. Why Selina indulged her at all this week was a mystery, because until now, she'd avoided Aubrey as much as possible.

Another moan sounded, loud enough that she could hear it in the kitchen. Well, apparently Sky or Mia just came. Aubrey grabbed her keys and her purse before she left the rental.

By the time she jogged up the steps to Selina's place, the front door was opening.

Selina stepped through the door, the sunlight bringing out violet notes in her relaxed pixie cut. The white tee she wore was cut off right above her belly button, a mess of red scrawled words over the fabric. Her ripped jeans and chunky black belt accented those full hips, and as she stepped closer, Aubrey got a view of the perfect ass that had sent her temperature spiking sky-high when they ground against each other last night.

"How'd you get ready so fast?" Aubrey asked, scratching her nape.

Selina's lips quirked. "Did you think I was lying around in bed? None of my housemates are up right now either, so I'll gladly get some breakfast." She cast a cursory scan over her from head to toe, and a flush crept through Aubrey. "Sidenote, you don't look like you're about to die."

"You don't understand my need for caffeine then," Aubrey said, shifting back and forth on her feet. At any point she could step into motion, needing to burn off the energy that zapped between them any time they were in proximity. They could probably fuel the country of Spain with this electric current. Selina's presence in any room just upped the voltage, whether from the witty comments that'd be incoming or the seductive way she moved. Fuck, Aubs was obsessed.

"Though." Selina cast her a sidelong glance as they set off down the sidewalk in the direction of the Silver Mug. "Now that you have my number, we'll have to discuss appropriate times. Daytime, sure. Three in the morning because your booty call left and you're lonely—that's a hell no. I'll be catching some well-deserved rest."

Aubs's chest twisted, like Selina was somehow able to peer into far too many nights Aubrey had returned to bed by her lonesome and wrapped herself in the cold sheets, the sweat drying on her skin like paste. Even with the remnants of the exertion, the soreness of her pussy, her swollen lips from the hookup, she had ached inside, still empty after those encounters. It wasn't like she could just switch gears though. The idea of committing again, of diving so deep in with someone only for them to ditch her at her worst—fuck, she couldn't survive dropping that low again.

"Hey, that's far too intense for pre-coffee discussion," Aubrey said, slashing her hands out.

Selina's brows lifted an inch, but she nodded. "Right, so about the gorgeous blue sky. Clearly, it's up to something conniving."

Aubrey snorted. "Very menacing puffy clouds up there. Dammit, Beckett, keep with that wit at all the best times, and I may have to call off this enemies thing we've got going on."

"I doubt enemies drag each other out for morning coffee," Selina responded, her tone cracker dry. Aubrey had come to relish the woman's brand of sarcasm and dry wit, so different from the doe eyes she was used to getting from women at the bar, at the gym, or even out at random restaurants. She'd always been drawn to challenges though, and Selina was the exact sort of catnip she didn't need right now.

The sign for the Silver Mug came into view, beaten iron scraps framing the black lettering, and the door swung open and shut with the steady stream of traffic, even this early. The closer they got to the door, the more Aubrey caught the murmurs of chatter inside and the scent of roasted coffee drifting her way.

Her stomach rumbled. "I need eggs and bacon, stat."

"Part of your training regimen?" Selina asked, the usual mocking grin departing for a soft curiosity.

"A lot of protein—yeah. Being a kickboxer requires burning a lot of calories, and you're expected to stay in a certain shape if you're an instructor. That's the reason I'm hauling ass at early hours even on vacation to go on runs. If I start slipping, it takes a lot of work to pack on the amount of muscle I need to kickbox."

"Thank God I just run a bar," Selina responded with a feline grin. "That sounds exhausting."

Aubrey reached the door first and held it open for her. Selina bobbed her head in a nod and entered, striding up to the hostess stand and asking for a table for two. A slight blush reached Aubrey's cheeks as she scanned over the other two-seaters in the room filled with couples. Because this was a coupley sort of thing she never indulged in. Maybe she'd grab a shake with a client or have a business meeting at a coffee shop, but morning brunch?

Off-limits.

Just like the woman slinking before her.

Aubs tugged on the end of her ponytail, wishing she wasn't such a damaged head case. Maybe then she'd be able to go on a date with a woman without feeling this crushing pressure, without those memories of Lila creeping in with the suffocating reminder. Was this a date? She'd hit up Selina for brunch, and the looks that kept scorching between them felt pretty damn date-like.

Even with the air conditioning on, a nice balmy breeze swept through the Silver Mug from the open windows. Selina skimmed her hand through her hair as she followed the hostess over to the two-seater stationed right under a hefty bushel of sunbeams. Aubrey settled into the seat opposite Selina, unable to help but soak in the vision of the woman before her. Christ, she'd encountered many, many gorgeous women, but none of them affected her like this.

With Selina, she didn't just get turned on—because hell, she left most of their interactions with her panties soaked—there was also this comfort around her she hadn't experienced in years. Like she could just... be. Like no one wanted anything from her, whether it was a good time in bed, loud, sassy entertainment, fitness tips, or the dozens of other things she got bombarded for on a daily basis.

"What are you going to eat?" Aubs asked, looking up from the menu.

The heat that flashed in Selina's eyes made her realize her choice of wording. She used the menu to fan herself a little, trying to not get overwhelmed by the idea of anything sexual with this woman. Fuuuuck. Mind out of the gutter.

"Probably just a cappuccino. I'm not much of a breakfast person," Selina responded, her lips curving into a grin, as if she knew the lurid thoughts flashing through Aubrey's mind right now.

Aubrey pounded the table between them. "Come on now, don't leave me to eat by myself. At least get toast or something."

Selina arched an eyebrow. "I suppose I could manage toast."

The waitress swung over before any more discussion could happen, and Aubrey placed an order for a large, large coffee and a bacon and cheese omelet. She was more than ready to devour some heavy protein. Selina ordered a cinnamon roll and a cappuccino.

Once the waitress walked away, Aubrey couldn't withhold her snort any longer. "You, a cinnamon roll?"

"Is there something wrong with liking sweet things?" Selina asked, casting her a warning glance.

Aubrey shook her head, even though her grin widened. "Nothing wrong with that—I just didn't take the Queen of Chill for the cinnamon roll and cappuccino sort. More black coffee and wheat toast."

"Just like you think I read serial killer novels instead of romance," Selina responded dryly. "What sort of monster did you fashion me into, sunshine?"

A shiver ran down her spine at the nickname. The moment it first left Selina's lips, she wanted to remember how that felt, the warmth that flickered through her at something personal from the woman, something belonging to them. She needed to shake some sense into her head before she continued to fuel this fantasy that wasn't going to happen. No way Selina would trust her after the woman had watched her work her way through her bar for years, picking up women left and right. That was where their antagonism started in the first place.

"I don't know, a splash of Freddy Krueger, maybe a little bit of Jason thrown in there for all the silence? I mean, we could elevate you to Mike Meyers," Aubrey responded at last, offering a cheeky grin. If only she didn't love winding this woman up so much.

Selina lifted a middle finger in response. Before Aubrey could say anything else, the waitress came back with her large mug of coffee and Selina's cappuccino. Even though steam wafted up from the mug, Aubrey lifted it to her lips and took a scorching sip. Anything to distract herself from the woman who drove her to deliriousness by proximity alone. Her phone buzzed, and she took a moment to check, in case it was Chels. Nope, just Kyle, with a thumbs up.

"Looks like Kyle got laid last night," Aubs responded, returning her gaze to Selina.

The woman drank from her cappuccino with a fitting elegance. "So what you're saying is the one person in your household who isn't getting some is you. I've got to say, that's a rather dramatic twist."

Aubrey shrugged, a sweep of vulnerability crashing over her. Truth be told, she hadn't gotten laid once on the vacation, and even with her worries about Mom buzzing in the background, she'd still managed to enjoy herself. All because of Selina Beckett.

"Maybe there's more to me than diving from one bed to the next," she said, trying for a joking tone. She wavered, her voice scraping. Right, that failed.

Selina offered a contemplative look as she sipped

at her cappuccino. When she placed the porcelain mug back on the wooden table with a soft thump, Aubrey couldn't pull her attention away if she wanted to. There was something about the woman's serious demeanor, the gravity of her presence, that anchored her there.

"From what I've seen, there's a whole lot more to you, sunshine," Selina said, all teasing leeched from her voice. "Maybe you weren't the only one who made a wrong assumption."

The flush reached Aubrey's cheeks this time, and she ducked her head. She'd never gotten this thrown off her axis before. "Stop with all the sweetness before I fucking melt onto the ground. I'm not built for kindness."

The words just slipped out, but she hadn't realized how true they were.

Selina's brows faltered, a flash of sadness skating across her gaze. Sadness for her. Aubrey scrubbed her face and drank another scorching sip of coffee, burning the roof of her mouth in the process.

When she looked up again, Selina's focus had shifted to someone walking in the door.

"Oh, damn" slipped from Selina's mouth.

CHAPTER EIGHT

Selina had been so focused on Aubrey that everything else drifted away, the other couples dining here, the waitstaff, the flicker of the light in the back that needed fixing—everything.

At least, until she happened to glance at the door at the exact wrong time.

Slender, chic, and naturally blonde, Katerina Leonard drew eyes everywhere she went. She'd caught Selina's once upon a time, and the year and a half they'd spent together had her dreaming of more permanent things.

At least, until she'd caught her in bed with the same raven-haired, long-legged woman who strolled in behind Kat. Bile rose in Selina's throat. A year had passed, a year filled with uneventful or downright horror-show dates and a whole lot of yearning, yet her scarred hurt opened like a fresh wound with the two of them standing in the same room.

"Everything okay, sweetheart?" Aubrey asked, her tone coming out concerned.

Right. She needed to pull herself together. Delaware was a small state, and while Kat avoided Renegades, she'd been living in Milton, a quick drive from Rehoboth. Selina could handle being in the same room as her ex.

"Just spotted someone distasteful, that's all," Selina responded through gritted teeth.

"Let me guess," Aubrey drawled. "Ex?"

Selina quirked a brow at her in response. "How'd you know? Was the loathing leaking out of my pores?"

"I'm guessing the breakup wasn't the amicable sort." Aubrey skimmed the crowd behind them as if she tried to gauge who it was.

"No, I'm not pointing her out," Selina said. The waitress swung by with their meals in the nick of time before Aubrey got the chance to ask any more questions. The last thing Selina needed was to slice herself wide open about Kat's betrayal to someone who avoided commitment like a second job.

Selina picked at the edge of the gooey cinnamon

roll, focusing on the simple task. The sweet vanilla of the frosting and the fragrant spices drifted up, tingling her nose. Aubrey drove a fork into her bacon and cheese omelet, shoveling the food into her mouth like she hadn't eaten in a century.

Selina took the first bite and savored the sweetness mixed with the cinnamon sugar of the roll, enjoying the way the flavors burst on her tongue. She'd been so focused on licking the sticky frosting off her fingertips that she almost missed the shadow falling over their table. Selina looked up in time to spot Kat and her—fucktoy? Girlfriend? Honestly, their relationship was none of Selina's business at this point, except for the fact that they stood here looming over her.

"Long time to see, Sel," Kat said, her voice soft and dewy, as if she was some fifties starlet.

"I'm fairly certain the distance was on purpose," Selina responded, trying to force her voice to remain level. Aubrey glanced between them, her gaze swinging back and forth like she was observing a badminton match.

"Just because we're split up doesn't mean things have to be bitter between us," Kat said encouragingly as her girlfriend slithered around her like a scarf. "I mean, I've moved on, and I assume you have as well."

Selina's heart wrenched at the comment. As much as Kat spoke in a dulcet tone, she'd always driven in barbs that way. A year had passed, yet Selina felt as lost and hopeless as she did the day she'd started packing her things to find a new place of her own. She'd moved on from Kat a long while ago, but she hated seeing her ex here with the woman she'd brought into their bedroom. What she hated even more was that she still roamed out into the land of ghosting and bad dates—and she struck out every time.

She glanced back up, realizing she should've said something by now.

"Excuse me," Aubrey jumped in, a spark in her eyes that Selina didn't trust. "I'm pretty sure she doesn't want to talk to you right now."

"And who are you?" Kat asked, lips pursed as if she kept her judgement in her back pocket.

"Her girlfriend," Aubrey responded, not backing down in the slightest.

Selina almost choked on her own spit.

Aubrey offered Kat a smile that almost looked malicious. "So, if you don't mind—you're interrupting our date."

Kat stared at Aubrey, and then her gaze returned to Selina—questioning, accusatory.

"She's not wrong," Selina responded, her tone cool. She wasn't offering the woman an out. "Hope you have a lovely breakfast." At that, she switched her focus to Aubrey, trying to ignore the wild beating of her heart.

Kat and her girlfriend made small derisive noises and strode away, heading over to their table. Selina didn't let out her breath until the pair had taken their seats. She may as well not have bothered at attempting to calm down, because the moment she glanced at Aubrey, the breath snagged in her throat again. The woman stared at her, lips pursed and a curious look in her eyes.

"Sorry about the whole declaration," Aubrey offered. She speared another bite of bacon and cheese omelet, chewing on it as she averted her gaze. "The woman was being a bitch and didn't have a reason to swagger over here and interrupt your morning."

Selina swallowed hard. She wasn't mad. Furthest thing from it. Instead, all she could think of was the possessive way Aubrey said "girlfriend," the strength of her proclamation, and the passion in her eyes when she declared it. Not like Aubrey Moore would ever stake an actual claim to anyone. Selina had yet to see it.

"Didn't bother me," she offered a half smile. "And you're right. Kat was flaunting her relationship for no other reason than bitchiness. Her girlfriend's the woman she'd been cheating on me with." Stating it out loud caused the shame to form a film on her skin, but after the way Aubrey came to her rescue, she wanted to explain.

"That's even more levels of fucked up than I'd anticipated," Aubrey murmured. "Are you sure you don't want me to march over there and deck her? I'd be happy to give my fists some nice test swings."

Selina snorted. "Why don't you save those prizewinners for better targets?"

Aubrey gave her a pointed glance. "I can't think of a better target. With how careful you are to let folks in, that sort of betrayal has got to be devastating. Say the word, sweetheart."

A flush rose to Selina's cheeks at Aubrey's honest affection, how she leapt to her defense even after all the time they'd spent squabbling. Despite the distance she'd been trying to keep, maybe she'd slipped a little too and revealed more of herself than normal.

"Thanks, pretend girlfriend. Let's save the beat-downs for another day." She took another sip of her cappuccino and a bite from the cinnamon roll, halfway finishing it. Aubrey had polished off her plate and sat there sipping at her coffee.

"Unfortunately, I think Kat and her girlfriend killed my already precarious morning appetite," Selina continued. "Do you want to get out of here? I've got a great place to walk off the calories."

"Of the half a cinnamon roll you ate?" Aubrey rolled her eyes. Still, she flashed a grin, all enthusiasm and charm, like nothing ever bothered her. "Though, you've said the magic word—please, whisk me away from this place."

Selina signaled the waitress over for their check, and before Aubrey could fight her, she offered the woman her card. She glanced back. "Is the magic word 'walk'? Because that's not helping your case as the human version of a golden retriever."

"Right, Catwoman. Find any more sunbeams to curl up under?" Aubrey shot back, a grin on her lips.

"Ha, hilarious," she said. Once the waitress returned with her card and receipt, she scooped them up.

Aubrey lifted the mug to her lips and chugged the remainder of her coffee. She placed an empty cup back onto the tabletop. "Lead the way."

Selina signed the receipt and left it on the table, sliding the strap of her black leather purse around her shoulder. She rose from the seat, not glancing behind her where Kat and her girlfriend sat and enjoyed their meal. Sure, maybe she should've stuck around to prove their presence didn't bother her, but their impromptu stop-by had soured her breakfast, and she'd rather not waste her time. She headed toward the door, and Aubrey kept a close pace behind her.

The moment they stepped out into the sunlight, Selina drew in a full breath again. Away from the suffocating gaze of her ex, she could think a little clearer.

"It's about a ten-minute walk if you don't mind the stroll." Selina glanced at Aubrey as she headed in the direction of Lake Gerar Park.

"Please, does it look like I mind a stroll?" Aubrey asked, flexing her biceps with a saucy grin.

Selina gave her the side-eye. "Don't see how those guns will help you, unless you're planning on walking over on your palms."

"Don't tempt me," she said, swinging her arms side to side. Already, she stepped a clip or two faster than Selina, as if she was about to burst into a jog. "Where are we heading?"

"You were that kid, weren't you," Selina shot back. This time of day, the boardwalk and beach were packed with families, but she and Aubrey just walked along, dodging the swarms as they wound their way forward. "The 'are we there yet?' kid."

"Whatever gave you that idea?" Aubrey smirked, her bright cockiness infectious under all of this sunlight. They continued on through the crowds until they'd begun to thin out.

"Just a sneaking suspicion," Selina responded, rolling her eyes. Even as she feigned annoyance, she didn't feel it for a moment. Had she run into Kat and her girlfriend while she was by her lonesome, she might've crumbled. She'd have strained an attempt at cool apathy, but the moment she stepped out of sight, she'd be heaving breaths like she tried to swim in the ocean. After the last hurt, she'd been careful—maybe too careful—with her heart.

Aubrey made all the difference today.

As much as she should be protecting herself, Selina couldn't help but spend more time with this beguiling woman. Every time she thought she had a pin on Aubrey, she found herself more confused. One thing grew clear—just because Aubrey slept around a lot didn't mean she wasn't loyal. The sort of loyalty she'd shown here today? Well, damn. Selina had been dreaming of a partner that fierce.

She slowed first, and Aubrey took the cue as

Lake Gerar glittered in the distance. "We're almost there."

Aubrey hooked her thumbs in her waistband as they walked, a distracting motion that placed some of her luscious tanned stomach on display. "What did you see in that chick in the first place?" she asked, glancing away and up at the blue sky as they strolled along.

Selina's heart stuttered at the personal question. It'd be so easy to circle around, to offer some witty response so the conversation could reroute to more comfortable territory. However, right now, her chest squeezed tight, like all of her unspoken pain was a wet rag begging to be wrung out.

She shrugged, rubbing her arms as if she'd been caught in a breeze. "Kat was my last foray into dating someone who'd picked me up at my bar. When we'd first met, she was charming and witty. She made me laugh, and in the time we were together, I thought she wanted the same thing I've always been searching for—somewhere to stay and someone to stay there with. I've spent far too many years watching the unfamiliar faces roll by as I hopped from one school to another, one state to a different one. It's exhausting and damn lonely."

Aubrey pressed her lips together, and she stared

at the ground as if in deep thought. Not like Aubrey would understand—from the gist of it, her family had been in the same place from high school and up. Army life had been so different, and while she loved her parents with all her heart, she'd been anxious to carve out a home for herself from the moment she turned eighteen.

"Doesn't Renegades give you what you already need?" Aubrey asked. "You know, a place to belong?"

Selina crooked an eyebrow at her. "Sure, but sometimes when I get home from a long shift, all I want to do is cuddle up with a partner in my warm bed, to be able to talk about my day with someone other than my cat. Sometimes, I'd like to make coffee for more than just me, or walk in the park with someone else by my side. We wouldn't need to talk, but the presence alone makes a difference."

The words spilled out of her, more than she'd allowed herself to confess in years. She'd been so focused on finding the right fit that she seemed to have evaded them at every turn. Here she was, nearing thirty and still searching, each failed date making her retreat a little further.

Aubrey let out a low whistle. "Damn, you almost make all the cozy shit sound enticing." She cracked a grin, attempting a carefree tone that faltered. For the life of her, Selina couldn't figure the woman out.

Lake Gerar sparkled ahead of them as they came closer and closer to the place she'd retreated to on many of her Rehoboth visits. Despite her fear of deep water, she found something comforting being around it. So often, when the others went to the beach, she'd sneak off with a book and sit by the lake, not nearly as chaotic or loud. This sort of place allowed her to think, to breathe, to relax.

"Funny, we come down here every year, and I've never been to this spot," Aubrey said, strolling beside her with purpose.

A question bubbled inside Selina, one that ended up slipping out. "What makes all the cozy shit so repulsive for you?"

Aubrey flinched for a moment, a visible streak across her face that quickly dissipated. Selina regretted the question at once. They'd been sharing more and more with each other, but each bit was a struggle.

"Despite appearances, I'm duck-feather slick, and all the comfy shit rolls right off me," Aubrey commented, a forced lightness in her voice.

Right. Avoidance games like normal.

Selina didn't respond but just stepped a bit

quicker toward the lake. They set onto the concrete walkway surrounding the lake, the gentle breeze causing slight ripples across the sparkling surface. While a few folks strolled around the perimeter fringed with pines and weeping willows, most of the place was isolated, the quiet as pristine as the beach at night.

"No one bothers with the lake when they came for the beach, which means I get to enjoy my outside time uninterrupted," Selina murmured.

"You really hate crowds, don't you," Aubrey said, a grin cracking her lips.

Her nose wrinkled in response. They continued to walk along the lakeside, the freshwater breezes intoxicating. With the sun beating down overhead and warming Selina from the inside out, the incident at the brunch place faded away like a distant memory. She wished healing was that easy, but at least she had her outlets. She glanced at Aubrey, who strolled beside her. The woman's pensive look didn't fit on a face usually filled with bright smiles and vibrancy. Selina lapsed into quiet as well.

They stepped underneath the fronds of a weeping willow, their shade creating an area ten degrees cooler. Selina came to a stop, staring out over the water. Aubrey's presence buzzed beside her.

"The cozy shit sounds nice in theory," Aubrey commented, her voice a low scrape. "But the crux of it is—once those comfortable times fade away, when things get tough, that's when you need someone the most. That's when they leave you. Why bother wasting time building all of those Kodak moments if they just cut and run when your life takes a turn for the worse?" She glanced at Selina, those russet eyes somber. "Any solutions? I'm all ears."

Selina found she couldn't look away. The raw pain emanating from the woman was more than she'd bared to her before, and the volume was deafening. Aubrey's dark eyes were glossy, the tilt of her brows so vulnerable and broken that Selina's heart cracked in two.

She found herself closing the distance between them to slide a palm against Aubrey's cheek. The way the woman leaned into the touch tugged at her chest like nothing else, and before she could talk herself out of it, Selina took a step in closer until her lips pressed against Aubrey's.

She tasted like coffee, her mouth warm and willing as their lips brushed together. Selina's head spun from the sheer intoxication of the collision, how every touch and connection between them inspired sparks. Aubrey's hand drifted to her waist, and she couldn't help but continue kissing this gorgeous, baffling woman. The kiss had been meant as a comforting gesture, an impulse she couldn't deny, but all too fast, it deepened.

Aubrey's grip tightened on her waist, and Selina slid her hand around to grab Aubrey's nape. They pressed their bodies together, the heat between them flaring brighter than the candles she lit for Yule. Selina couldn't help but fall into the ferocity of this kiss, even though she was the one who'd initiated it. Aubrey took control with ease, dragging her tongue across Selina's, claiming her mouth like she owned it. The sheer possession in her movements sent Selina reeling, her knees trembling. If not for Aubrey's grip on her waist, she might capsize.

This felt inevitable and terrifying in the same sweep, like the drop of a rollercoaster, yet Selina couldn't pull herself away. She memorized the softness of Aubrey's lips, the sharp taste of her, the power behind her movements. The woman's magnetism was clear from the start, but oh, Goddess, the way she kissed. The confidence she commanded with her mouth left Selina helpless to the onslaught, and she just wound her hands around Aubrey's nape as they kissed and kissed and kissed.

They separated for air, the sounds of their breath

coming out in violent bursts after the fierce way they'd come together. If that was how Aubrey kissed, Selina couldn't imagine how she fucked. Her panties were soaked.

The separation allowed the first thoughts to infiltrate, the ones that should've snuck in before.

Bad idea. Bad idea. Bad idea.

Selina took a step away, and the spell began to dissipate, despite the way her pussy throbbed and her lips tingled. She couldn't do this. Not with Aubrey. She'd already been hurt far too much.

"Right, we should head back," Selina said, before Aubrey could continue. She glanced away, needing to put some space between them and fast. "Our roommates are probably wondering where we are."

"Lead the way," Aubrey responded, her voice coming out a little hushed, a little breathless.

Selina started walking as fast as her legs could carry her.

CHAPTER NINE

Aubrey had spent the rest of the day with the crew, heading to the beach and splashing around in the waves. Ky was glowing from her potentially more than one-night stand, and Sky and Mia were all sweet kisses and soft whispers with each other, which left Aubrey to her thoughts.

The thoughts that continued to circulate around one individual: Selina Beckett.

She sat at the breakfast nook of their rental, tapping her fingers along the flecked granite surface. Ky stood at the skillet, prepping a late lunch or early dinner for them, though she trusted Ky the least in the kitchen out of all of them. Luckily, burgers were hard to fuck up—though she'd seen Ky burn pasta before, so her hopes weren't the highest. Mia was taking a shower while Sky lounged on one of the powder-blue couches lining the living room.

She hadn't planned on slipping into feels territory like she did back at the lake. Truth be told, she didn't do that with anyone, not even her closest. Only Ky knew details because she'd been there through all the tough stuff, but somehow the swaying limbs of the weeping willows, the gentle freshwater breezes, and Selina's calming, quieting presence coaxed the words out of her.

On top of that, she hadn't expected the kiss—or how much the kiss would dominate her mind. Aubs had experienced a thousand and one of them over her lifetime, and honestly, the past few years they all melded together, none sticking out. However, Selina's kiss wasn't just a jolt to her nether regions, kick-starting her core to life. Sure, she could've wrung out her underwear after kissing that woman once, but goddamn, the whole thing was so much more.

Locking lips with Selina Beckett was like the first time she'd taken a kickboxing class—an exhilarating thrill of an epiphany that felt right when nothing else did. Kisses like that—connections like theirs—didn't exist in real life. At least, that's what she'd believed.

"Did someone roofie you, Aubs?" Sky called over from the couch, looking up from the glob monster of a fantasy novel she was reading. "I'm pretty sure this is the quietest I've heard you in years."

Ky arched a brow. "Noticed you weren't here when I came back. What did you get up to this morning?"

"Grabbed breakfast so I didn't starve, since all of my friends were getting lucky instead of me," Aubrey said, rolling her eyes. She hoped that was enough to keep them from noticing the flush creeping up her skin, but with Ky's eerie powers of observation, you never knew.

"I'd offer to be your wingwoman, but Mia and I planned tonight as date night," Sky said, resting her book on her thighs. "We could always go out tomorrow instead? Only a few nights left on vacation, and I don't want you feeling lonesome."

"Nah, I do better solo anyway," Aubrey said, waving a hand. Truth be told, her chest squeezed tight when she thought about changes that had happened on their trip. Watching Sky and Mia together disrupted the norm and sent her a bit off-kilter, as did the concerns over Mom. Those worries had simmered on the back burner through this entire trip.

"So, you don't mind if I go out with Kim again?" Ky asked, her question tentative. "I feel like we've barely spent any time together this vacation." Behind those words brewed her best friend's worries that would only get extinguished once hers were—if she found out her mother didn't have cancer again.

"As if we don't go out together most weekends." Aubrey attempted a reassuring grin. She'd been so focused on hunting for scraps of time with Selina and ignoring the health issues her mom was going through. Spending time with Kyle brought a lot of painful memories to the forefront, just because her best friend had been one of the few there with her through the whole battle the first time. "Ky, enjoy yourself. You've found a gorgeous woman to spend some time with. Out of everyone, I'd never fault you for that."

"Listen to her," Sky called out from the couch. "How many times has Aubs ditched us to go chase some tail?"

Aubrey jerked a thumb at Sky. "What she said."

Ky gave her a pointed look because the woman was way too discerning. She'd have questions and want to know specifics—like what was going on between her and Selina. Truth be told, Aubrey didn't have the slightest answer.

All she knew was that she wanted to see her again.

Aubs pulled out her phone and shot off a text. *Want to hang tonight?* She left her phone out on the counter, impatient for a response already, even though she'd just sent the text.

Kyle chewed on her lip as she darted around the kitchen, grabbing the hamburger buns, cheddar, ketchup, and mustard they'd picked up from the nearby grocery store. A second later, she let out a low curse and raced over to the skillet to flip over the burgers that had begun to waft a charred scent through the kitchen.

Aubrey's phone buzzed. *Only if we're clear this isn't a booty call.*

As much as her libido thrummed at the idea of picking up where she'd left off with Selina, she wanted the escape offered. When she was around the woman, Aubrey's mind quieted, which was a rare and uncommon feat.

I'll keep my hands to myself. Scout's honor.

Her phone buzzed back moments later. *Why do I get the feeling you were never a Scout?*

Aubrey couldn't help the grin that rose to her lips. Fuck, this woman turned her upside down.

"Dinner's... ready?" Ky said with a wince, plating out charcoal-dark burgers that the melted cheese desperately tried to slide off of. Aubs tried to cover her snort as Sky hopped up from her seat to join them.

"Let's eat."

Everyone had ventured out their separate ways once night arrived. Sky and Mia headed to some swanky seafood restaurant, while Kyle and her date were going to a different club to dance this time. As for Aubrey, she hadn't made any plans beyond swinging next door to bother her temporary neighbor for the five thousandth time.

The house was quiet since everyone had already left, and she took a moment to readjust her sporty red dress that came to mid-thigh. She swore her allegiance to several sportswear brands, Athleta being one of the tops, and most of her clothes, even items beyond her athleticwear, came from there. She'd taken the time to apply some makeup—just a streak of eyeliner and mascara along with some gloss.

This wasn't a date. Not really. Fuck, Aubrey didn't even know what was going on between them, but she found herself wanting to look eye-catching tonight. She'd do anything to draw Selina's gaze again, even if she had to keep her hands to herself.

She grabbed her purse and slung it around her shoulder. Her keys jangled in hand as she headed for the front door. The moment she stepped outside, the night-sweetened salt breeze drifted her way, far cooler than it had been during the day. She hopped down the steps two at a time until she reached the pavement with a clap of her flats and strode in the direction of the rental next door. When she stopped in front of the stairs, she caught sight of Selina chilling on one of the wicker chairs, legs crossed.

Even in the yellow-green glow of the outdoor light, Selina looked next level gorgeous. Her full lips were glossy, and the mere sight had Aubrey squeezing her legs tight at the memory of how good they'd felt against hers. Selina wore a short, pleated skirt that came above mid-thigh and a gray tee that fit her far too well. Her chunky silver jewelry caught the moonlight.

"If I whistle, are you going to send me away?" Aubrey teased as she sauntered up the steps.

"The temptation's high." Selina's brow crooked, every motion she made so delicate and controlled. With how out of control Aubrey felt most of the time, she found something about the woman's precision undeniably attractive.

"Question of the night, though—where do you

want to go? We've got our pick of bars, restaurants, or none of that. I'll let you decide, Miss Fancy Bar Owner." Honestly, she was hoping Selina had a clue what to do. When she'd messaged her, she hadn't made any plans, and the trend continued right up through her walk over. "Just letting you know though, I've already eaten. Kind of."

At least, if the charred remains of burgers counted as a meal.

Selina's lips quirked. "Would you hate me if we spent some time by the boardwalk and the beach rather than cramming into a building? The ocean's too pretty at night to pass up."

Aubrey couldn't help but recall their walk on the first night here, her heart thudding hard. Out at a loud bar or restaurant, she could easily drown out the sheer need percolating through her veins after that kiss, but alone with Selina? That was like running straight into a burning building.

"Sounds good to me," Aubrey's mouth answered for her before her brain could make a better decision. Trying to keep her hands off of Selina tonight would be an agony, especially with the way her skirt slid up her desert-colored thighs. Fuck, restraint would be agonizing.

Selina pushed up from her seat and strode on

past her, those mesmerizing hips swaying with each movement. This close, Aubrey caught her scent, all orange blossom and amber. The fragrance ignited her. God, everything about this woman was delicious, and Aubrey wanted to taste her more than ever. Truth be told, she wanted to splay Selina out on this deck, hike up that flimsy skirt, and fuck her with her mouth until her screams could be heard down the street.

Right. Head out of the gutter.

Aubrey shook her head and followed Selina down the creaking steps as they headed along the sidewalk toward the bustle of the boardwalk. The whole place was lit up neon in the evening, big beams from the spotlights illuminating everything.

"What were your other friends doing tonight?" Aubrey asked. Somehow, they'd managed to spend most days and nights together on this vacation, and her friends had picked up on the fact for sure, even if none of them said much outright. Her mind refused to chew on the implications of spending so much time with Selina when the most Aubrey ever offered someone else was a single night.

"Cass and the others wanted another bar night, and you know how much I love those," Selina said with a shrug. "My illustrious plans had been to spend the night with a book until you texted."

Aubrey nudged her in the side with her hip, keeping pace with her. "What, with the whole buffet Rehoboth has to offer?"

"I'm willing to go on dates, but I've owned Renegades for too long to want to pick up women at a bar. I've seen that scenario over and over again, and after several of my own failed attempts, I got myself out of the game. Besides, it's not a great business practice to do that at my own joint."

"Is that how you met your ex from earlier?" Aubrey asked, curiosity overtaking her. Standing this close to Selina tortured her. She was dying to reach over and slide her arm around her shoulders.

"Bingo," Selina said, a bitterness ringing in her tone. "And she wasn't the only one. Every time I've tried that route, it always ends up being a flash flood that leaves me wrecked."

As they neared the boardwalk, the sounds from the crowds grew louder, the lights flashing down on them. Normally, Aubrey reveled in the chaos, but she'd found herself intrigued by the contrast Selina offered. She was someone who walked in peace and solitude amid lonely lakes and empty night-darkened beaches.

"So, are we bypassing this scene and heading straight for the beach?" Aubs asked, curiosity getting the better of her. She hated making plans, even though she had a thousand and one opinions. Yet Selina seemed to always have an idea tucked into her back pocket, and so far, they'd all been new experiences for Aubrey, a contrast from the rinse and repeat of different girls at different bars every week.

"One stop first," she said, a glimmer of amusement in her gaze. Those dark coffee eyes were gorgeous, lined in kohl and so subtly expressive Aubrey found herself sneaking more and more glimpses.

Up ahead of them in bright, blinking pink neon lights was the candy store, and Selina slowed her footsteps. Aubrey wanted something sweet, but she craved it more from the woman swinging those pendulum hips in front of her.

"You want us to get sugar highs before we take to the beach?" Aubs asked, unable to keep the skepticism from her voice.

"I haven't picked up any saltwater taffy yet, and you look like you need something more than whatever you ate for dinner. I thought I caught smoke coming from your kitchen," Selina commented as she walked through the doors.

The bright lights barraged them at once, along with a medley of sugary scents.

"Saltwater taffy's the worst though—there are far better things out there," Aubrey commented as Selina made a beeline for the towers of pastel and neon-wrapped taffy.

The woman turned around to shoot her daggers. "You take that back, Aubrey Moore."

Aubrey rolled her eyes, even though a grin snuck onto her face. "Never." She headed over to the section with chocolate and grabbed a few chocolate peanut butter cups, bringing them over to the register. Selina slipped by her side a moment later with a plethora of multi-colored taffy in a bag.

"I've got hers too," Aubrey said as she jerked a thumb to Selina. To her surprise, Selina didn't argue. The woman at the register nodded, ringing them up quick, and they were off on their way again, heading back out into the velvety darkness.

Aubs blinked a couple of times when they exited because the lights inside the shop were so bright, but after a few paces, they made it off the boardwalk and onto the beach. The soothing salt breezes wrapped around her, sending a shiver down her spine. She'd tucked her bag of peanut butter cups in her purse, saving them for later. Selina, on the other hand, had already unwrapped one of the taffies from her crinkly bag. Aubs couldn't help but watch as the woman lifted it to her lips and closed her eyes to savor the taste.

Great, she'd reached the point of sexual frustration that she was jealous of taffy.

"What's the allure of the beach for you if you don't like the water?" Aubrey asked, still curious. Every time she got to know more about Selina, she found herself surprised by what she learned.

"Have you seen this place?" Selina swept an arm out. "Just because I'm terrified of getting dragged away by the riptide doesn't mean I can't enjoy how intense and powerful all of this is. When it's quiet on the beach, you can appreciate the roar of the surf and the way the moonlight glitters on the waves. The landscape is so different from the loud plastic pails, warring umbrellas, and tons of sunbathing bodies that comes with the beach during the day."

Selina didn't talk much, but when she did, she was mesmerizing. Aubrey balled one hand into a fist at her side, her nails biting into her palm in an effort to not reach out. She'd agreed to be good. She could be good. Until they'd kissed earlier, she'd been able to dance around the idea of anything physical, but they'd cracked open that shaken soda bottle, and now that need was a steady tap, tap, tap through her veins.

Selina glanced over at the fist she'd made. "Going to lob a punch at someone?"

"Oh, I always walk like this," Aubs said, attempting to be casual, as if she wasn't going crazy in Lustville over here.

Selina crooked a brow. "I've got a solution. Want to try some taffy? I bet I can change your mind."

Aubrey snorted. "You're going to have to try hard. I've tasted the stuff for years and never once has it had any allure."

Selina finished the piece she chewed on and turned to face her. Before Aubs could click two and two together, Selina leaned in and pressed her lips to Aubrey's. Her fingers swiped over Aubrey's balled fist, loosening it as she kissed her. Once Aubs recovered from the surprise, she sank into the kiss. Selina's warm tongue swept into her mouth, bringing with it the sweet tang of the saltwater taffy.

Aubrey nearly let out a moan. She'd been holding back from the moment she saw Selina tonight, but then the woman made the first move. The clever, beguiling, and stunning minx. She rested her palms on Selina's hips, gripping them tight as she kissed her with all of her pent-up lust and longing.

Heat flushed through her at the feel of Selina's body pressed against hers, and Aubrey couldn't help but take the lead, gliding her tongue along Selina's as she deepened the kiss.

A hesitant moan escaped Selina's lips, and Aubrey swallowed it up, desperate for anything this woman might give her. She'd never met anyone more challenging in her life, and as they stood before the boom and crash of the ocean before them, she understood a little more of how rare that was. How Selina transported her to this calm, immense place at once, no matter where they were. Her pussy throbbed, and her nipples ached, brushing against the fabric of her dress as she dragged Selina's body flush to hers.

In her eagerness, she stepped on a slope in the sand, sending them both off-kilter. Aubrey's reflexes saved the day as she grabbed Selina tight and they tumbled to the sand. Selina's back hit the ground, and Aubrey crouched over her, their breaths heaving. Her thighs surrounded Selina on either side, the brush of skin to skin nearly making her delirious. For a moment, she stared into Selina's eyes, dark and enticing like the blackened waters in the distance.

Selina's tongue glided along her lower lip. "Just kissing." The words were firm, even though her eyes flared like unspent coals.

"That I can handle, sweetheart," Aubrey responded, her voice husky with desire.

Her legs splayed around Selina's, their bodies an inch from crushing together. She spread her palms in the still-warm sand on either side of Selina, and she couldn't help the thrill that rushed along her spine. The moonlight gleamed in Selina's eyes and high-lighted the sharp jut of her chin and those knife-edge cheekbones. The woman was so beautiful it made Aubrey's head spin at the feeling of their bare legs touching where Selina's skirt was hiked up her smooth thighs.

Her breath puffed against Selina's, mingling with the sweetness there. Aubrey sank down to capture the woman's mouth in a kiss again. Her breasts crushed against Selina's, and between that and the way their bare legs tangled up on this sandy beach, her underwear was soaked. God, this woman turned her on like nothing else. She speared her fingers through Selina's hair as she memorized her mouth, leaning down on her elbow as they continued to find each other's lips again and again and again.

In the distance, the boardwalk buzzed with people, but behind them, only the tides stood witness, an undulating crash and roll as they lapped onto the shore. Aubrey mimicked their rhythm, unable to pull herself away from Selina if she wanted to.

The more kisses she coaxed from those lips, the more she never wanted them to end.

If only Aubrey was meant for more than one-night stands and summer flings.

CHAPTER TEN

———————

Selina moaned explosively as her back hit the wall of the bathroom stall.

Aubrey had been true to her word over the past two days since their beachside make-out session—kissing only, but goddamn, each round since that first one left Selina breathless and needing far more time with her vibrator than before.

Aubrey's lips caressed her neck as the woman pinned her against the cool surface of bathroom stall, and she couldn't help but surrender. Selina closed her eyes and let the sensations wash over her. Her core throbbed, and her pulse quickened in the wake of the way Aubrey bit, nipped, and sucked at the column of her neck. She wrapped her arms around Aubrey's shoulders, and the woman's hands remained on her hips with a settling grip that let her know who was in charge.

She'd always suspected Aubrey Moore would be unforgettable at this sort of thing, but the reality shattered her expectations. The scent of lemon and sage lingered around her like pure sunshine. Aubrey smelled fresh and vibrant, filled with so much life. Aubrey's lips crashed into hers again. Their mouths tangled in a collision of tongues and teeth. They kissed like this might be their last one, chasing every final sensation together.

Selina's lips grew swollen, and the taste of sweet rum lingered between them along with the metallic tang from the fierce way they crashed together.

This excursion had been unintended. Selina had gone out to the bar with the girls, but the moment Aubrey and her crew showed up, her former plans got jettisoned into the sea. Ever since they'd kissed the other day, neither of them could get enough. They'd both made every excuse to slip off and find a secluded corner to make out, whether it was behind her rental or in one of their cars. This time was no different.

"God, you're so fucking hot," Aubrey moaned against her mouth, pinning Selina in place with her body, her palms settled on her hips like she owned her. If this version of Aubrey was the only one she'd met, Selina would've offered herself up in a heartbeat. She'd been waiting ages to feel this zip of attraction again, for her synapses to fire to life like she'd been rebooted.

"Back atcha, gorgeous," Selina purred between kisses, their breaths coming out like minor explosions. Her shoulders heaved, and sweat beaded on her skin like they were in here for a different reason. Not like she'd indulge in sloppy bathroom sex with anyone. As much as she'd let herself go here—she had her limits. Their lips brushed against each other a few more times, as if they were trying to siphon out any lingering bits of pleasure they could.

Selina's pussy throbbed to the point of distraction, and the temptation grew fierce to let this go to its natural conclusion. But she'd spent her earlier years indulging in meaningless hookups, and they'd always left her feeling hollower in the aftermath. At least she could draw her line here and hope her heart wouldn't be aching for too long when the vacation ended and they both went their separate ways.

Their kisses grew slower and more deliberate as they savored each one between breaths. Aubrey tasted gloriously sweet, the heat emanating off her body bringing Selina close to combustion. She could feel how Aubrey restrained herself from going further, and that alone settled her every time they made out. Not like she was absolved from thoughts of Aubrey's sensual mouth between her legs, her hands on her thighs spreading Selina open. A vicious ache throbbed in her core, and she locked lips with the one woman who could do something about it.

The bathroom door creaked open as someone came in to use one of the stalls. The sound snapped her out of her reverie. Not like anyone was surprised by two women together in a stall at a gay bar. She did her rounds at Renegades when lines began to form, rattling on doors to get any hookups moving along.

Selina forced herself to pull back, even though she could lose herself in those gentle kisses just as much as the desperate ones. Aubrey's lips were as swollen as hers, strands of her hair plucked out of her ponytail and her slim white shirt rumpled. The red skirt she wore was hiked up her thighs in a way that was far too inviting.

"We should head back before the others suspect something," Selina murmured, keeping her voice low.

Aubrey snorted. "I'm pretty sure the bathroom excuse didn't convince anyone, sweetheart."

Selina gave her a look. "Well, I promised them at

least a little time tonight, and I intend on giving my friends that."

Aubrey's grin softened. "Sounds like a plan." She unlocked the door, and they both headed toward the single mirror overtop of a worn sink.

Selina popped on the faucet, splashing some icy water over her face, as if that could even attempt to smother the flames roaring inside her body right now. She took a minute to swipe her relaxed strands into place and straightened the form-fitting tank top she wore so her bra no longer peeked out the top.

Behind her, Aubrey straightened her clothes as well, pulling out her hair to redo her ponytail. Selina couldn't help the glance back at the gorgeous woman, noticing how even in the sallow bathroom lighting, her tan skin looked bitable, those defined muscles on clear display. Her chestnut hair shone with some visible golden streaks as she gathered it back with a hair band again.

Selina dug into her pocket and found her lipstick. She applied a fresh layer since Aubrey had kissed away all the gloss she'd been wearing. Maybe this shade of plum could hide the fact that her lips were swollen from their intense make-out session.

Not like she'd be able to dismiss it from her mind easily.

Tonight would be long and restless in her lonely bed.

Once Selina finished applying lipstick, Aubrey leaned in beside her so their hips nudged together. "You realize that shade on your lips makes me want to kiss you all over again."

A flush spread across her cheeks. "You're insatiable, sunshine."

To her surprise, Aubrey pulled back, but not before Selina caught the blush staining her cheeks. Something about making this cocky, indomitable woman react felt like a victory, and she couldn't help the way her heart sang in triumph.

"All right, let's go mingle," Aubrey said, grabbing the door and pulling it open.

Selina sauntered out first, scanning the crowd for Cass, Steph, and Zane. They hung on the opposite end of the bar, but she caught sight of Cass's gaze landing on hers, slight surprise in her umber eyes. Even after taking the time to straighten up, she felt like she wore a blinking sign above her head that pointed out what she'd just been in there doing. Part of her wanted to indulge right now, caught in a vacation spell, but the other part of her, the sensible part, understood she had set herself up for heartbreak.

The first day back at Renegades when Aubrey

showed up and whisked some winsome blonde off her barstool would be pit-in-the-stomach misery that would linger for a long time.

Aubrey waved over to where Ky sat at a table alongside Sky and Mia, not too far from Selina's friends. This was where they should part ways and spend some time with the people they'd arrived here with instead of drowning in each other.

They hadn't even gotten several paces past the bar when a voice sounded behind them.

"Aubrey? Selina? Is that you?"

Selina turned around, a prickle of discomfort spreading through her. A woman sat at the bar behind them, her blonde hair back in a pin-tight bun and her mauve dress so snug it might as well have been plastered on her. Selina focused for a moment, trying to place where she knew the woman from when the realization hit her like a smack. Renegades, of course.

"Hey, Ria," Aubrey said, her voice a low, tentative scrape. The woman's grin widened at the sight of them, her bubblegum pink lips and infectious smile belonging in a Crest commercial.

"Go figure I'd run into the two of you down here, and even in the same room," she said, a lilt of amusement in her voice. "Don't you guys hate each other?"

"Ah, yeah, definitely," Selina attempted, even though her voice sounded fake to her own ears.

Luckily or unluckily, Ria didn't seem to process that in the slightest. She hopped off her seat and placed a hand on Aubrey's shoulder. "Must be fate running into you here."

Selina's stomach twisted. Jealousy was the exact thing she couldn't handle, not when zero trust had been built between her and Aubrey. The woman never made any promises of changing, and Selina should've known better than to indulge.

"Probably more of the fact that we're both living in the same state and hitting up the hotspot most lesbians do," Aubrey commented, her shoulders stiffer than normal. Discomfort radiated off her, which came as a surprise to Selina, who was used to seeing Aubrey descend into slick and charming at the drop of a hat.

Ria stood in front of her and dragged the tip of her pointer finger down Aubrey's chest. "I know you don't do repeats, but I hoped you'd make an exception...," she purred. "Vacation and all."

Selina swallowed hard. She needed to put some space between them—*now*. "Great running into you, Ria," Selina said, taking two steps forward. "I better be getting back to my friends." Not like she could take standing there and listening to them flirt in front of her. After all, why wouldn't Aubrey go for Ria? The woman had all but flung herself at Aubrey, and unlike Selina, she was willing to go for the whole sweaty one-night spin in the sheets.

Selina could vaguely hear Aubrey's voice behind her, but she tuned it out as she quickened her pace, heading toward Cass and the others. Christ, after all of that, she needed to tip back a pint more than ever. Selina forced her gaze forward, refusing to look back as she carved her way through the busy bar. She settled into place at the open seat by Cass. Steph and Zane had already gotten up, making their way to the bar for drink refills.

A quarter of her pint of porter remained, so Selina strode up and tossed back the liquid. Cass's eyes burned into her, but she didn't look her way until the pint glass hit the table with a thump. Selina couldn't bring herself to glance in Aubrey and Ria's direction. She didn't want to witness any of their interaction.

"So, care to explain why the woman who avoids players at all costs just stepped out of a bathroom with the biggest one in the state?" Cass asked her, drumming her fingertips on top of the counter.

"Don't suppose you'd believe a bra malfunction?" Selina tried, her throat drying as she attempted to ignore all the nerves rearing up after the dose of reality. Seeing Ria from Renegades was like a sign from the Goddess that she shouldn't be pursuing anything with Aubrey, even casual make-out sessions. Truth be told, as much as she'd chalked up everything as casual, none of it had been. She didn't go for moonlit walks or kiss on the beach with her friends, and the heavy tension between her and Aubrey had grown with every encounter.

"Hey, if you decided to have yourself some fun, you know I'm not going to rag on you about this." Cass's voice softened. Her friend had known her ever since she'd arrived in Wilmington, which counted for one of her longest friendships, considering she'd never stayed in a zip code long enough to keep anyone. "I just worry, because I know you."

"Don't worry—I set my limits," Selina murmured. Not like those made a whit of difference when her heart was on the line. "You know I wouldn't fuck a random girl in the bathroom."

Cass pursed her lips. "If Aubs was capable of changing her ways, I'd say dive in, but I mean, hell. The girl over there is eyeing her up like the Lucky Dragon Buffet, and she's not running for the hills."

Selina forced her gaze to follow, even though her

chest already sank. The initial meeting was bad enough, and she didn't need to see the vision in real life that she kept replaying over and over in her head of Aubrey grabbing Ria by the hand and leading her out the door.

When she glanced up, however, Aubrey patted Ria on the shoulder before she turned in the opposite direction. Ria pouted playfully before she found her seat by the bar again, but Aubrey didn't look back as she sauntered toward Sky and the others at their table. Before she made it all the way there, Aubrey's gaze flickered in her direction and held, a flare of accusation there. Selina returned her stare, her chin jutting out since she refused to back down. What was she supposed to think when that had been Aubrey's MO from the moment they met?

"Well I'll be damned," Cass said, taking a sip from her martini. "Apparently hell has frozen over, because for the first time in her life, Aubrey Moore turned a woman down." Her gaze drifted over to scrutinize her. "I don't suppose you have anything to do with that change? I've noticed how much time you two have been spending together."

"Who knows," Selina muttered into her empty glass. "I'm not taking too much stock in it. We're on vacation, after all."

Cass opened her mouth as if she might say something, but Steph and Zane wandered over, so she closed it.

"Just in time for drinks," Steph said, carrying an extra porter over and placing the drink in front of Selina.

"You're an absolute doll," she responded, settling back into her seat with the porter in hand. She spared another glance in Aubrey's direction, but to her continued surprise, the woman sat in the booth with her friends, laughing and cracking jokes rather than swooping through the bar on the hunt for a woman to take home. Selina's battered heart made a hesitant thump of hope, one she tempered with the reminder that this was temporary.

For the next hour, she sipped at her porter and enjoyed drinks with the others, for once no one rushing off to their own agenda. She got the itch for nicotine however, and once she finished her drink, she got up and headed out front for a smoke break.

Selina sucked in a deep breath of the salty air, unable to help how it transported her mind to just the other night as she'd tumbled around the beach with Aubrey. A full body flush surged through her, and she grabbed the pack of smokes, smacking the flat part against her side before she plucked one. In seconds, Selina had lit her cigarette, and she drew in the first blissful drag, one she needed after the Wild Mouse roller coaster she'd been dragged through tonight.

A moment later, the door creaked open.

Selina caught the scent of lemon before Aubrey settled beside her against the wall.

"For someone who doesn't smoke, you sure take a lot of smoke breaks," Selina murmured, trying to settle her nerves. After the way she'd bolted earlier, she didn't want to dive deep. If anything, she wanted to go running in the opposite direction.

"I'm starting a new thing," Aubrey commented with a sideways smile that made Selina's heart thump a little harder. "Fresh air breaks. I'm pretty sure the trend will take off."

"Going to head out soon? Ria looks like she's in search of a warm bed," Selina commented, wishing the words didn't make it feel like claws were sinking into her chest.

"Think I'm that easy, do you?" Aubrey asked, her voice deepening with an irritation they both felt. "Any bed will do?"

"You tell me," she challenged back, heat flooding through her.

"I'm interested in locking lips with one woman

tonight, and it's definitely not Ria," Aubrey growled, stepping in front of her. God, that note of possession just about killed her resistance.

Selina sucked in one more drag from her cigarette before she dropped it to the ground. Aubrey took another step in closer until Selina's back was flush against the wall. Once Aubrey's lips slid against hers, she closed her eyes and surrendered to the sensations.

Tonight was proof this could never last, but she'd enjoy every second while it remained.

Two days.

Two days until this vacation ended and Aubrey had to return to real life. God, she didn't want to. Aubrey's ponytail bounced as she trekked along the asphalt on her morning jog. Unlike all of her other times on the annual Rehoboth trip, she hadn't gotten laid yet. Normally, she might care, but every time she was around Selina, she forgot why that was even an issue. Every adventure, every interaction endlessly engaged her, and she couldn't help but circle back around to Selina, like she was magnetically propelled.

And she needed the distraction more than ever. Mom was back at home based on what Chels said, but they were waiting on the results from tests.

Which meant her return home might also vault them back to that time—moping around in the hospitals, visiting Mom and Dad's home, and watching her vibrant mother turn sallower and weaker every day. The first time had been bad enough. She didn't know if she could survive a second round in the ring, or hell, how Mom could.

Aubrey continued to jog around the block, wondering if she might see Selina on the porch again when she neared her rental. The woman draped herself over the wicker furniture with a book any spare second she could. The sun pounded overhead, and sweat trickled down Aubrey's back and her fore-head. Her breaths came out sharp and hard from the punishing pace she raced along at, trying to work off some pent-up frustration. Ria had thrown herself at Aubrey last night, and any normal time after a dry spell, she would've jumped on the strings-free hookup.

Something stopped her.

Someone.

The moment Selina stepped away to head over to her friends, the idea of taking Ria up on her offer just felt slimy, like she'd slicked up her arms in oil. How the hell did she get this tangled up? She'd spent years breezing by from woman to woman, bed to bed, and yet once she started connecting with Selina on this vacation, her traitorous heart wanted more.

The sun beat down on her bare skin, her shorts hiking higher up her thighs as she ran. Strands of her ponytail plastered to her sweaty back, but she kept pushing herself along the asphalt, needing to feel the burn.

Selina made her imagine the one thing she hadn't allowed herself for years—the cozy fantasy of returning home after work to someone waiting for her. To shared kisses, shared beds, and shared Christmases with the same partner.

Funny how that crept up right when her mom might be getting sick again. Her stomach lurched, and she struggled to hold back the memories of how Lila ditched her when things got hard. She'd been with the woman for a year, and they'd been just as disgusting as Mia and Sky. They'd curled up nightly on the couch in their apartment, just basking in each other's company. Aubrey had planned their whole future out, not a thought to anyone else, but when faced with one big hardship, their relationship was a porcelain doll hurled to the asphalt.

Those insidious questions had begun to arise with Selina—what if she was the same?

What if she wasn't?

Aubrey didn't know if she could face either. Maybe keeping it to kissing was better, because if she sank any deeper into this woman, she didn't know how she'd begin to extricate herself.

She slowed her jog as she neared the house, her heartbeat rattling in her ribcage as she searched the front porch of the rental next door. Looked empty, and as she passed, there was no sign of the hottest bar owner in the state lounging about with a book. Disappointment pulsed through her, something she loathed. How had she become this attached?

Aubrey hopped up the steps to her own rental, which still emanated a soft, airy quiet at this time of the morning. She strode through the kitchen and turned a faucet on, splashing some cold water onto her face post-run before she filled a glass and chugged the contents. Even in the wake of all that exertion, her mind raced just as much as it had before she'd begun.

Her phone started buzzing on the table, causing her brows to draw together. Who would call her this early in the morning?

She flipped over her phone, and the moment she caught Chels's name on the screen, her chest sank.

That couldn't be good.

She snagged her phone and answered the call,

heading back outside. Not like she wanted to have this conversation where any of her friends could hear.

"Hey, Chels," Aubrey said. "What's going on?" She thundered down the steps as she turned to the right side of the house and found a shaded spot along the wall to lean against.

Chelsea sucked in a sharp breath. "Aubs," she murmured, her voice sounding watery. Aubrey's alarm bells were clanging.

"What's going on with Mom?" she asked, unable to keep the sharpness from her tone. Worry spiked like an EKG.

"She's back in the hospital again," Chelsea responded, even though the words came out halting amid the occasional sharp breath. "She was feeling dizzy and almost passed out again, so they had her come back in. No one's able to figure anything out, and they're still waiting on all the damned tests."

"They've had all week and they can't get some fucking blood work results?" Aubrey asked, anger scorching through her. "What's going on at Christiana Hospital that they're so behind?"

"I don't know," Chels muttered, her words still thick even as she tried to rein in her fears. "I'm just worried. And every time I try to talk to Noah about it, he's been shrugging me off."

"Well, fuck him," Aubrey spat back. "Not literally, because he's a dick. But Chelsea, your husband can be an almighty douche sometimes. Marriage is in sickness and in health, and that extends to your parents who might be suffering."

Just more proof why marriage was for idiots and commitment for fools. Not like she'd say that to her little sister who'd accepted the engagement proposal after six months of dating. Aubrey might not like the guy, but she'd never try to make Chels feel like shit. She had a useless husband for that role.

"I just... what if the cancer's back again?" Chelsea asked, her voice barely skating above a whisper. "I can't—she can't handle that again...."

Aubrey leaned against the cool siding of the house, trying to ignore the stinging in her own eyes. As if that hadn't been what ran through her head on repeat this entire trip. "Want me to come up? I can relieve you at the hospital," Aubs said, determined to do what was necessary to be there for Chels, even though her shitty husband wouldn't.

"You're coming home in two days though, right?" Chels said. "Why don't you take the weekend shift?

That would help me a lot more than you rushing up here and cutting your vacation short."

"Is Noah going with you?" Aubs asked, even though she knew the answer in her gut.

Yet another reason why her original plan of flings only was the right one. Partners never stuck it out through the tough times. The moment life got difficult, they'd start distancing, or they'd outright ditch.

"He's too busy right now to join me, but it's okay. I'm there with Dad, so I'm not by myself."

Like being with Dad would be much of a solace. Silence remained their favorite shared pastime, since Aubrey refused to stop being gay and he wouldn't stop being a bigot. Mom was the one she'd always melted around, the parent who'd accepted her no matter what and still tried to get Dad to see reason. Chels was the golden child in his eyes though—the straight one.

Fuck, the hospital visits before had been excruciating. Not just because of watching Mom fade, but because of the rift between her and Dad that would never get mended.

"Babygirl, hold on right now, okay?" Aubrey said, sliding into the big sister role she'd never forgotten. "I'll be home in a few days, and you can crash at my place one of the nights and we'll have a big vent session—just get all of this out."

Chels gave an audible swallow before she responded. "That sounds good, Aubs. Thanks for... being there."

"Thank you for keeping me updated through this," Aubrey responded. "Lord knows our folks wouldn't if they had it their way. None of that 'don't worry about me' martyr bullshit."

"It's bullshit all right," Chels said, sounding a little steadier. "Have a good rest of your vacation. And call me when you're on your way home."

"Give yourself a break today. Take some time to rest, okay?" Aubrey said, rubbing her free hand along her forearm.

"Will do," Chels said, before she hung up. Aubrey tipped her head back to stare at the blue sky overhead, far too perfect for the miserable turn this day had taken. When she'd gotten the news Mom could at least head home from the hospital, she'd thought maybe. Maybe she was okay.

The return to the hospital felt all too familiar, and right now, Aubrey couldn't stomach it. Though, truth be told, she didn't know if there could be any time she'd be able to process Mom's life in jeopardy. Again. She heaved a sigh and pushed off from the wall to stride back inside the house. She didn't bother looking over at the rental next door. Aubrey wasn't in the right frame of mind to deal with anyone right now, especially not with the confusion involving Selina.

She stepped back inside, the cool air pumping from the overtaxed AC as she headed toward the kitchen to fix herself some breakfast. Coffee. Things that might make her feel a little more human.

Footsteps creaked behind her, and she bit back a curse. She wasn't great company right now, even for best friends.

Ky strode up beside her and picked one of the eggs from the carton. "What do you want to bet I can burn scrambled eggs too?"

"Which is why I'll be handling breakfast, thank you very much," Aubrey said. "I'd like something not charred in my stomach."

Silence spread between them as Aubrey set to work, not rambling like usual. She could feel Ky's stare burn into her, but she chose not to respond.

"So when are we going to talk about this thing between you and Selina?" Ky broached, and Aubrey physically bit back her groan. That was the last thing she wanted to discuss right now while her head was clouded like she'd downed Nyquil. "Because to me, the situation's looking far less casual than your usual flings. I mean, the whole dipping into the bathroom or sneaking outside together is nothing new, but I don't think I've ever seen you this focused on one woman before. At least not since...."

Don't say it. Don't say it.

To her relief, Kyle didn't continue, just stared at her with curiosity.

"I'm allowed to switch things up once in a while," Aubrey said, attempting to be cavalier, even though her irritation leaked out in the process. "Doesn't mean I'm about to sweep Selina off her feet and propose."

"I'm not saying that," Ky responded, huffing out a breath of frustration. "Aubs, I love you. This isn't me trying to attack you. I'm just saying you're allowed to like someone. You're allowed to fall for someone. The world isn't going to end."

Except her world might.

Mom might have cancer again, and this time, she might not survive.

Aubrey flipped the eggs on the skillet, and her jaw clenched so hard it might crack. Her hands began trembling, and she prayed Kyle didn't pick up on it. The observant asshole probably would.

The words wouldn't arrive on her tongue. All of

those thoughts were sealed too deep inside. Ky knew the waking nightmare of stale hospital lights and pitying sympathies from every random acquaintance Aubrey had dealt with the last time Mom went through chemo. Throughout, Kyle Walker had been there, a loyal, steadfast friend. Aubs should tell her what was going on. Hell, maybe she should even tell Selina.

Except all she could hear was the tremor in Chelsea's voice and the resignation there when Noah failed to show time and time again. She'd already lived through that disappointment and wasn't prepared to set herself up for it again.

No one signed up for this struggle, and she and Chels wouldn't abandon Mom. Sure, Selina might be okay with listening to her woes one night and walking on the beach with her—a vacation escape was easy.

But the hospital visits? The countless breakdowns in the middle of the night? The freeze-ups every time the phone rang as she awaited the worst?

Hell, even she didn't want to go through that again.

"Falling for someone was never in the equation for me," Aubs said, fighting to keep her voice steady. "Vacation's almost over, Ky, and I'm returning to the norm. We both know what that means."

Ky's lips formed a thin line, but she didn't argue. She knew the deal with Aubrey's mom, that they didn't know what state her health would be in. And summer flings were that for a reason—because the moment Aubrey returned to reality, all of those pressures came crashing down.

No matter how much Selina's presence calmed her or how being around the woman opened up doors she'd shut years ago, she needed to quit this. Before she fell any deeper.

Aubrey couldn't afford attachments, not with the reality awaiting her in just two days.

CHAPTER TWELVE

Selina was going to murder Cass's meddling ass.

When Cass saw Aubrey turn down Ria at the bar the other night, she'd become convinced the woman had gone through a miraculous change and that Selina and Aubrey were soul mates meant to be together forever. Her enthusiasm made Selina's skin itch—mostly because her hopeful heart begged her to allow those same feelings to roam unbridled.

However, she'd always been too pragmatic for that.

Yet, because of Cass's meddling, they were going out to the bar with Aubrey's crew, one big celebratory party, since after tonight, they only had one more day of vacation. The conclusion of the trip loomed in her mind, a far bigger ending than returning home from a week of ocean breezes and sunny reads.

Part of being a pragmatist meant she didn't waste too much time deluding herself.

She'd already begun to fall for Aubrey and hard.

No matter the limits they'd placed on things, every time she was in the same room with the woman, her heart had begun to accelerate like she'd hit the freeway and jammed on the gas. And she'd begun to fantasize about what could happen if Aubrey changed—if she was willing to give this connection between them a chance.

The sign for Castaway Cantina stood out overhead as she waited in line with Cass. Tonight, Steph and Zane were having a date at the Oyster House to celebrate the last full night here, so she and Cass were on their own to do what single women did in Rehoboth—troll the bars in the hopes of finding themselves a wild night.

Except Selina would be around Aubrey yet again. Those first kisses had just been flirting with flame, but the deeper her feelings grew, the more the fire began to take hold and spread until an entire forest got caught in the blaze. She tugged at the chunky bracelets weighting her wrists, wishing they'd tethered her to some common sense in the first place. Either way, her traitorous heart hadn't taken the memo.

When Aubrey turned down Ria to spend the night with her friends and then came out to find Selina later, the butterflies had threatened to consume her. They'd avoided the talk up until now because Aubrey never made any promises, and Selina hadn't harbored any delusions... at least, before.

Now, her mind was traveling years into the future without her permission, her heart hopping on a flight while she couldn't even get to the airport.

She skimmed her fingers through her hair and smoothed her skirt instinctively. She'd gone with a slouchy crimson tunic and a short black skirt, busting out her eighteen-hole Docs.

"You're going to wingman for me tonight before you go off and make out in whatever shadowy corner you can find with your lady love," Cass said, the closer they got to Castaway. "I'm sick of going everywhere solo."

Outside of the bar, folks lingered to either catch a smoke or chat under the lamplight, everyone engaged in casual conversation. The murmurs threaded through the sea air, and in the distance, she could hear the quiet lap of the tides to shore, steady and undulating. Selina focused on the sound to calm the jitters sneaking through her at the thought of spending yet another night with Aubrey.

"I can handle that," Selina murmured, wishing she had a belt or loops to grip onto—something to occupy her hands. After tonight, she had one more day until she'd be relieving Heather from bar duty. If she didn't have a bar manager she trusted, she would never be able to take this trip in the first place.

"You're not mad that I invited them with us tonight, right?" Cass asked, glancing her way.

Selina sighed and shook her head. "I'm not mad. Conflicted, confused, and all of that mess, sure, but I know your heart's always in the right place."

"I just want you to find happiness," Cass murmured, nudging her in the shoulder. "I'd be content with a good lay, but you've been so patient. You've tried so hard to stick to your guns, and you deserve a happy ending more than anyone I know."

Selina squeezed Cass's shoulder. "As if I could love you any more. You know you're going to find what you're searching for too."

Cass offered a hesitant grin, her dark eyes dancing. She tugged on one of her careful braids. "Someday, I hope."

Chatter poured out of the constantly opening door of Castaway Cantina, along with the throb of electronica. Even from here, she caught the scent of tart lime from the abundance of cheap margaritas on the specials menu tonight. Selina's heart sped the closer they got to the door. At the beginning of this week, she'd been bored out of her mind in this bar, and Aubrey Moore had been a big warning sign of "avoid at all costs." One talk outside of here changed all of that.

They stepped inside, and the blast from the AC greeted them first, followed by the dim lighting and the thrum of a packed bar. Part of Selina wanted to bolt in the opposite direction at what felt like a Saturday night at Renegades, but the other part of her searched the crowds for any sign of Aubrey.

It didn't take long to pinpoint their group. Aubrey and the others had taken a seat at the back of the bar, all wedged around a few tall tables with stools to accommodate everyone. Aubrey was dressed to kill in ripped jeans and a shortened tee that exposed her delicious abs. Selina couldn't help but recall the feeling of those curves pressed against her, and how Aubrey had strength enough to pin her down. The fantasy of the woman lifting her up and fucking her snuck into her head quite a few times, along with about a dozen others.

Every make-out session left Selina panting for more—which might never happen. All she'd have would be the scorching kisses and quiet moments they'd shared. In truth though, that was far more than she gave to most.

Aubrey lifted her molten gaze and pinned her to the spot. The air may as well have evacuated the room. Selina smoothed her hands along her skirt again, as if that might help. The intensity threatened to consume her, but by some miracle, her feet continued to carry her across the bar in their direction. Cass zeroed in on her a couple of times followed by a knowing smile, but she just weathered the looks. She knew she was barely keeping her usual cool.

As she got closer, Selina sucked in a steadying breath. They stopped in front of the tables and claimed the open stools.

"How many drinks deep are you guys in?" Cass asked, dropping her elbows to the table. "I'm planning on letting loose tonight."

"I'm going to drink the bar dry," Ky muttered, staring into her margarita. "My fling from the other night decided to fling herself in the arms of another woman."

"Back into the pool with the rest of us, eh?" Aubrey said, elbowing Kyle in the side. Selina's stomach twisted at the comment, but her steady gaze didn't flicker. "Unlike the gross almost-married couple over there."

Mia stuck her tongue out at Aubrey, and Sky shrugged, her arm comfortably wrapped around Mia's shoulders.

"I'll grab a refill for anyone who needs one," Selina offered, needing the breather. "Cass, what are you drinking?"

"Whatever's on special," she said, beginning to scan around the bar.

"I'll come and help," Aubrey offered, a wicked glint lighting her eyes. Something reckless had surfaced tonight, something that set Selina on edge. She hadn't spent years observing people to miss the subtle signs.

Aubrey slunk up beside her as they headed toward the bar. "You look fucking delicious tonight." Her voice was husky as her breath hit Selina's ear.

A shiver traveled down her spine—this was the cocky, self-assured woman she'd been avoiding for years because she was dangerous as hell. However, this version had never swayed her in the past, not until she'd seen the softer side to Aubrey that existed beneath all the arrogance.

"And you look like you're destined for a cold shower," Selina teased, reverting to autopilot.

"I'm pretty sure my dildo's going to run out of batteries after the past few days," Aubrey commented, a conspiratorial grin reaching her lips. Something felt off tonight, like the tender, loyal, and protective woman she'd gotten to know had been locked away in a tower, and Selina didn't trust the current facade.

"Lucky for you, there are convenience stores and loose women everywhere," Selina drawled, unable to help herself. Even still, her heart squeezed tight.

As much as she wanted to indulge in the escape Aubrey offered, she'd withstood the temptation to take things to the next level for a reason. She didn't toss around sleeping with people easily, and her long-standing rule was she only had sex in relationships once the emotional groundwork had been laid. Not like it saved her from heartbreak, but the opposite would corrode her over time.

Selina leaned over the bar to order a pint, two margaritas, and a rum and coke for Aubrey, trying to ignore how the woman scrutinized her.

She cast a glance at Aubrey. "Did something change?" she asked point-blank. "Back home?"

Aubrey's gaze shuttered, the expressiveness in her eyes blanking out. "Nothing that can't wait until the end of vacation."

Right. That explained the closed off version she'd received tonight. Every time she got close to cracking the code with this woman, Aubrey would throw in a twist, and Selina felt like she stood on wet sand that changed with every whim of the tide.

"Let's get these back to the crew," Selina said before any more questions slipped from her lips. She turned on her heel, but she could feel Aubrey's heated presence close beside her as they carved their way over to everyone.

She set the margaritas in front of Cass and Ky before she slid into place beside them. Aubrey slipped in on her other side, the flash of a challenge reflecting in her gaze. Mia leaned forward and glanced between the two of them.

"I've got to say, you guys are adorable. I didn't think I'd ever see Aubrey tied down," Mia said, her eyes shining with genuine warmth. Her expression socked Selina in the chest. Beside Mia, Sky winced and tugged at her arm.

Aubrey's gaze darkened. "You're going to be waiting awhile on that one, Mia B."

Selina schooled her face, even though the violent jerk inside hurt.

Aubrey pushed up from her spot at the table. "It's about time I started casting nets for the night too. Maybe I'll catch up with the rest of you later, or maybe I won't." The tone of her voice affected charm, but the coldness underneath could freeze the entire group. She didn't look Selina's way once as she hopped up and made her way to the bar.

The ice infiltrated to Selina too, coursing through her veins and numbing out those hopes that had started to emerge.

"Oh fuck," Mia murmured, glancing toward Selina. "I thought.... I'm so sorry."

Selina couldn't feel anything. Aubrey's switched mood dropped onto her like an atomic bomb, and her hopes for the night, for the vacation—period—were destroyed in the wake.

Cass reached over and placed a hand over Selina's, even though she could barely feel it. "I'm sorry too. I just wanted to see you happy. I thought after the other night that maybe she was different."

Selina lifted the pint to her lips, unable to process much else. She was still reeling, and the temperature had dropped to subzero for the rest of the crew.

Ky leaned forward. "If it makes you feel better, I can go over there and challenge her to a fight. She might collapse from laughter alone."

Selina attempted a smile that faltered. "Sweet of you, Kyle, but I didn't hold any delusions about changing her."

She dragged her gaze away, but in the process caught one sight in her peripheral that made the situation even worse. Aubrey leaned in at the bar, talking to a sweet redhead with perky tits who lapped up the attention.

This was the exact nightmare she knew would come. It just was a bit sooner than expected.

She shouldn't have gotten attached.

She shouldn't have allowed herself to fall.

The quiet at the table was deafening as everyone got really fascinated with their drinks to try and avoid the awkwardness seeping into their pores.

"So, what are your plans for the last day of vacation?" Selina forced out, by some miracle keeping a tremor from her voice. Sky met her gaze and nodded, seeming to understand her need to get out of this discussion and fast.

"Probably going to spend it by the ocean again.

Did you know less than five percent of the world's oceans have been explored?" Sky dove in headfirst, and Selina could've kissed her for the reroute. The moment she started spouting out weird oceanic facts, Mia caught on and redirected the conversation. Cass gave her hand one last squeeze before diving in to chat with the rest of them.

Selina did her best to avoid looking toward the bar, not wanting to inflict the sting of the lash on herself with every glance. Even still, the temptation was tearing her apart. The chatter at the table faded to noiselessness around her until all she could hear was the heavy thump of her heart in her ears. None of the girls bothered her, since they seemed to understand that she needed the space right now. Selina continued to lift her drink to her lips, even though she barely tasted the porter gliding down her throat.

Focus. One breath in. One breath out.

This hit harder than running into her ex at the coffee shop, even though she and Aubrey never made any promises. The cold chilled her from the inside out. They'd never discussed anything about the potential for a relationship, because deep down, she'd known that would send Aubrey running into the arms of the closest willing woman. Beneath it all, she hadn't been able to help indulging for once, even though this summer fling would wreck her.

Selina glanced up as if her gaze were being magnetically drawn.

Aubrey slipped her arm around the redhead, leaning in so her lips almost brushed her ear, charm written all over her features. The redhead stared at her, blue eyes drenched in lust. Selina's breath snagged in her throat. Her pulse slowed, and the movement around them seemed to cease.

Aubrey and the redhead pushed away from the bar, and together, they made their way to the door.

She was going to be sick.

"I need a minute," Selina murmured as she stood from her seat. She couldn't even feel her legs move beneath her, but somehow she floated toward the bathroom just in time to watch the door click shut behind them.

She slipped into the first empty stall she could find, her fingers trembling as she tried to tug on the handle. Selina slid against the cool surface, her legs barely keeping her upright. Once she locked the door behind her, the first tears slipped down her cheeks, hot, spiteful, and unrelenting. Her shoulders shook with silent sobs, ones she covered with her mouth as everything she'd held back slipped out.

Spending time with Aubrey, getting to know her, and allowing her in—it had all been a mistake. All of the back-and-forth comments, shared glances, and tender words all shattered like a crowbar to a mirror.

The tears continued to stream down her cheeks as she leaned against the bathroom stall, cracked wide open.

She should never have let herself fall for Aubrey Moore.

CHAPTER THIRTEEN

THE ONLY THING AUBREY KNEW WAS THAT SHE had royally fucked up.

When Mia referred to them as a couple, her internal alarms started clanging, and her throat tightened. She didn't have any answers, and the thought of what she'd be facing in a mere day or two took a mortar and pestle to the remaining hopes of anything between her and Selina.

However, what she hadn't been prepared for was the slime coating her insides the moment she walked away. When she chatted up Nina, the hot redhead at the bar, all she could think of was Selina sitting back at the table and the way her expression had shifted— how the light had shuttered out of her beautiful russet eyes. Aubrey had fought through revulsion to keep a smile plastered on her face.

Every time she glanced toward the table, a newfound guilt dripped through her insides. She and Selina made no promises, no commitments. She'd ditched friends dozens of times to go hit up a hottie at the bar, but it never affected her in the past, even when other women she'd slept with were in the room.

This—the acid pit in her stomach, the constant thoughts of Selina, and the hollow grins she kept offering Nina—this felt like cheating.

Which was why once she left the bar with Nina, Aubrey had done the unthinkable. She'd kissed her on the cheek, wished her a good night, and they went their separate ways. After the move she'd pulled, she couldn't go back into the bar with everyone else, but she only had herself to blame on that one. She was a flimsy plastic pail of mixed-up emotions and she was unprepared to deal with any of them right now.

She adjusted her hunched position on the steps of the front porch—not of her rental, but Selina's.

A few hours passed, enough time to cement things in her brain a little better. She didn't know the future, or really, anything beyond this vacation. But what she and Selina shared on this trip had been unique. The connection between them had been the most she'd allowed herself in a long while, and she couldn't hurt Selina more than she already had. The idea of any sort of conversation made her want to spew across the steps, but she could be honest.

Her ass had begun to grow numb, but it was a fitting punishment for being such a dickbag back at the bar. How hard would it have been to state the truth to Mia? That she didn't know right now? Fuck, if she hadn't gone to such lengths of avoidance to begin with and just admitted she and Selina had something undefined going on, they could've skipped all the awkwardness. But instead, she'd spent all week skirting around any conversations with Mia, Sky, and Ky about both Selina and the state of Mom's health.

Every time Aubrey spotted a figure at the end of the street, her gaze zeroed in, and her heart began to beat a little faster. She should be distancing herself right now—avoiding Selina for one more day before she returned home—but this throbbing pain in her chest refused to abate, and she knew the cause.

She lifted her head again, homing in on the short, curvy woman weaving her way back to this direction. Aubrey's mouth dried. All the reasonable things she planned on saying evacuated her brain. As the woman came closer, Aubrey's gaze snagged on the details—the hot-as-fuck black skirt, the crimson tunic overtop, and those fuck-me boots that turned Aubrey on from the moment she caught sight of her.

Selina headed her way, and it'd be a miracle if she gave her five seconds after the spectacular way Aubrey had fucked things up back there.

She froze in place on the stoop, unable to push herself up on her traitorous legs. The closer Selina got, the more it felt like icy claws sank deep into Aubrey's chest, giving her the thrashing she deserved.

Selina's gaze landed on her, and she stopped mid-stride, feet away.

"Wrong house, Moore," Selina said, her voice sharp and cutting. "Yours is one over."

Aubrey swallowed hard. She deserved that, she did. But seeing the cold frost over Selina's eyes caused her stomach to seize. "Look, you have every right to tell me to go the hell home and not hear me out," she started, trying to summon her courage. "But if you're willing to listen, I'd like to explain."

Selina settled in front of her, standing with her arms crossed. Aubrey couldn't help but notice that her eye makeup looked lighter, smudged as if she'd been crying. Fuck. Aubrey was such a damn monster. The should'ves threatened to bury her, but she couldn't do anything about them now. When Selina didn't speak and didn't try to bulldoze past her, Aubrey took her cue.

"I never went home with the chick in the bar," Aubrey admitted, clutching her knees. She dug her fingertips in, forming crescents in her skin. "I never wanted to either. When Mia called us out, I freaked. The entire time, it just felt wrong with you sitting on the opposite end of the bar and me standing with someone else."

Selina hadn't said anything, but she also hadn't left, so Aubrey kept going. "Look, I wish I was normal enough to promise you the world, but I'm still a little fucked in the head, clearly." Aubrey stared hard at her fingernails. "However, the one thing I can offer is a little honesty."

She glanced up at Selina, and the woman's arms dropped to her side. A moment later, Selina plunked onto the stoop beside her, staring out at the street ahead of them. Aubrey followed her gaze, the inky asphalt threatening to devour her like these wild emotions already had.

"I didn't always jump from bed to bed," Aubrey started, even though her breath hitched. It felt like she was peeling back her skin, the pain so acute she could scream. "Back when my mom first got diagnosed with cancer, I had a longtime girlfriend named Lila. We'd been together for a year, and I was sure she was the one. We'd go the long haul, get married, and settle down together."

Her throat dried, and she paused for a moment, not knowing if she could continue. She was wading into acidic territory where she might end up disintegrating in the process. Selina sat a little closer, her knee bumping against Aubrey's. The gesture alone gave her the courage to keep going.

"My mom's fight got really bad. We were pretty sure she wasn't going to survive, and when the hospital visits got longer, tempers strained. Everyone signs up for the good times in relationships, but no one wants to stick around when life gets hard, you know? Lila decided midway through that she'd had enough. There was no discussion. One day, she just disappeared, leaving a note of explanation."

Aubrey had returned from an overnight stay at the hospital with Mom, bone-tired and wanting to collapse into bed with the love of her life. Her skin permeated with the disinfectant and sick smell that coated her like tissue paper. The moment she'd opened the door to their place, everything felt different—off-kilter. Aubrey's empty mug still sat on the coffee table where she'd left it, but patches were missing from their place—Lila's favorite painting had been taken off the wall, the stack of her recently folded laundry had vanished, and a chunk of her DVDs and books were missing from the shelves.

Aubrey hadn't been able to comprehend any of it —the dizziness swirled through her, mixing with the sleep deprivation. She'd plunked down on the burnt orange couch only to see a handwritten note left on the coffee table.

Lila had brought some of her things with her on the initial drive—the rest, she'd picked up later. "Too hard" was the pair of words that haunted Aubrey ever since. They were the words that followed her for her entire life, from her father and from friendships over the years. This rejection was the final shred of evidence needed for a conviction. She was too hard to deal with, too much. She carried too much baggage.

Aubrey shrugged, trying to ignore the fact her hands trembled. "I've sworn off of relationships ever since. I learned a whole lot of self-reliance, and I always have Ky and Chelsea for when things get rough. Look, I don't know what's unfolding between us. I can't make promises because I don't even know where I'll be a week from now, or if I'll be stuck inside the never-ending hospital cycle or not." She clenched her fingers into a fist to stop them from shaking. "I just want you to know this week's meant something to me. That you mean something to me."

Aubrey let out a deep exhale, everything spilled out in the open. She couldn't bring herself to look at Selina—if those eyes were cold and distant like the stars tonight, she might break. The quiet buzzed in the air between them for a moment, but then Selina's finger slipped beneath Aubrey's chin, tilting it up.

"I'm still pissed for what you did in the bar back there," Selina murmured, those dark eyes ensnaring her. "But I think I understand a little more. We didn't set limits, and we didn't talk about any of this. However, even I recognize this whole opening up thing isn't something you offer to everyone."

Aubrey shook her head. "No one else." Her voice came out soft, hushed. The reality shocked her like a snowstorm in July, but she hadn't opened up like this, fully opened up to anyone in a long, long time. Somehow, she'd gone from sharing the burden to shouldering it alone until she nearly collapsed under all the weight. Selina cupped her face, her palm hot against her skin, and Aubrey sucked in a deep breath to keep back the heat threatening to overflow from her eyes.

"So, I'll set the boundaries here," Selina murmured. "One night and one day left of this vacation, and I don't want to spend it with anyone else, even if that's all you can give. You should never have left with another woman tonight, but I was only jealous because I wanted you to be leaving with me." Selina's eyes were somber, like they were capturing the moonlight and reflecting it back out. "Here's the deal. We have the rest of the vacation to explore this as much as we want. And I know I do."

"Why would you even want to spend time with me?" Aubrey asked, her voice scraping. "Hell, I'm still mad at myself after the shit I pulled tonight."

"Right now, I'm hopped up on jealousy and irritation I need to burn off," Selina responded, her lips curling in a feline grin. "We could either scream at each other to argue it out, or take the much more satisfying alternate route."

Aubrey licked her lips instinctively, her pussy throbbing at the liquid desire pooled in Selina's eyes. Fuck, she wanted this woman so badly. She didn't know where they'd stand a week from now, or even where she'd be. All she knew was that she didn't want to pass on this chance to be with the one woman she'd allowed in after so, so long.

Aubrey leaned in, brushing her lips against Selina's in a kiss. The moment the woman's mouth opened to hers and she softened against her, Aubrey dove in for the kill, drinking in the kiss like she needed it to breathe. The scent of amber and orange blossom made her ache, revving her into overdrive as she claimed those velvet lips. She sank into the bliss of the connection between them, the touch more electric than any in years. She could live off these kisses alone, but right now Aubrey burned with the need to imprint deeper, to leave an indelible mark on the woman who'd come to mean so much to her.

She broke away for breath. "One question," she murmured, their breath mingling between them. "Your room or mine?"

CHAPTER FOURTEEN

Selina had been prepared to send her away.

The moment she strode to her porch and saw Aubrey Moore sitting there, she'd wanted nothing more than to blow past her and lock the door tight. However, Aubrey had done the unthinkable—she'd opened up in full, confessing the past hurts Selina never thought she'd be privy to. After witnessing the raw pain in Aubrey's eyes and knowing she never went home with the girl from the bar, Selina came to a single resolution.

Aubrey might not be able to offer more when they returned home, and that might scrape shards off her heart, but this vacation belonged to them from beginning to end. If Selina only had her for this summer trip, then maybe she could accept the temporary happiness while she grasped onto it.

She stepped into the house, hand in hand with Aubrey as she guided them past the open floorplan kitchen and living room toward the steps. She and Cass had each claimed one of the upstairs rooms, which afforded them plenty of privacy. Midnight hues stained the white staircase, painting everything in shades of lavender and navy. Aubrey gripped her hand a little tighter as they reached the top of the steps. An intense awareness settled over her with the realization that yes, she was going to do this tonight. Mere hours ago, that wouldn't have been a consideration on her horizon... but things had changed far more rapidly this week than she could keep up with.

They stepped into Selina's room, ocean-scented potpourri heavy in the air. Her bed was neat, and her belongings remained in the suitcases, apart from a few books strewn across the floor.

Selina's confidence was a match that lit the moment she sat on the bed and soaked in the sight of Aubrey.

The woman looked so gorgeous standing there before her, midriff bare below her crop-top paired with skintight ripped jeans that Selina wanted to peel off with her teeth. The guarded version of

Aubrey she'd run into at the bar earlier was everything she hadn't wanted, but this? This was the real woman behind her bravado, a soft rawness emanating in the air between them. Aubrey's eyes filled with wonder as Selina's gaze rolled over her from head to toe.

Selina reached up to tug Aubrey onto the bed with her. Instead, Aubrey leaned over her, pressing her palms into the mattress as she skated her lips over the exposed skin on Selina's collarbones, trailing kisses over the fabric of her crimson tunic. Aubrey's lips traveled down a bit lower, closer to Selina's core. Her panties were soaked at the promise of those steady kisses, and her short skirt hiked even higher up her legs.

Aubrey sank to her knees in front of her, and Selina leaned back, barely able to catch her breath.

"The second I saw you tonight, all I wanted to do was rip this skirt off and devour you," Aubrey said, her voice husky with desire. Those words drenched her, and Selina's heartbeat picked up speed. The sight of the gorgeous woman on her knees with her mouth inches away from Selina's pussy and the knowledge that they were separated by fabric alone caused her entire body to light up.

Selina hadn't been lying—she'd been burning

with adrenaline and jealousy, but the moment Aubrey opened up, all of those hot, demanding feelings were directed elsewhere. Aubrey met her eyes, tilting her head questioningly. Selina nodded, propping herself up by the elbows.

"You're the most gorgeous thing I've ever seen," Aubrey murmured, pushing Selina's skirt up higher. She hooked her finger on the waistband of Selina's panties, and she dragged them down her legs, taking her time even as she maneuvered around the knee-high boots. The deliberate actions put Selina in the spotlight, but after all they'd bared together, this felt like the final step.

"Want me to take them off?" Selina asked, nodding to the heavy eighteen-hole boots she wore.

Aubrey shook her head, an impish grin on her face. "Hell no, sweetheart. Those are fucking hot."

Once her panties slipped to the ground, Aubrey settled between her legs, her hands resting on Selina's thighs. Her pussy quivered in anticipation. She'd grown so slick the moment they walked upstairs, and the sight of Aubrey on her knees sent a flush cascading all the way through her. She'd imagined this dozens of times, but now with the reality in front of her, all doubts and fears vanished—just pure anticipation remained.

Aubrey leaned in, the puff of her breath against Selina's folds enough to send her reeling. Goddamn, this woman was a fantasy. Selina's elbows dug deeper into the mattress as she strained to watch. Aubrey's grip on her thighs tightened, a confidence in her hold that made her feel secure. Her lips descended, and Selina couldn't hold back the moan that ripped from her. Aubrey lapped at her in long, slow strokes, everything so deliberate and controlled that each motion sent a pulsing thrill through her.

Most of the time, she never experienced this comfort, the ability to surrender to a partner until well into a relationship, but she and Aubrey had hopped onto the fast lane of getting to know each other this week. No matter what happened from here on out, she understood the woman just as much as she had any of her exes.

Aubrey opened her up with her tongue, lavishing attention onto her swollen clit. Each stroke sent sparks rolling up Selina's spine. Her thighs tightened, her hips lifting to meet Aubrey's mouth. The woman looked so damn hot between her legs, those dark, seductive eyes gliding up and down her body even as her mouth dominated her. Selina dug her fingers into the sheets, gripping them as she rode the pleasure that continued to build. The ocean breeze rolled through the window she'd left open, and Selina closed her eyes in abandon.

Selina moved her hips in time with Aubrey's demanding mouth as the woman nipped and sucked at her swollen clit until she was ready to burst. The sheets were cool beneath her, but a layer of sweat coated her skin as her breath hitched.

"More, sunshine," Selina purred, unable to help the neediness in her throat as she fisted the sheets.

Aubrey continued with a punishing pace against her clit, her tongue thrumming against the sensitive flesh until a scream stuck in Selina's chest, begging to break free. The tension mounted, closer, closer, closer, like she fumbled through the dark waiting for the burst of light to crash down. Her breaths came in shallower as Aubrey's relentless onslaught threatened to overtake her.

Aubrey squeezed Selina's thighs as she drove her tongue against her clit in one ferocious swipe that sent her tumbling over. Her clit pulsed as the orgasm swept over her in one blinding tidal wave. Selina tightened her grip on the sheets, her thighs trembling as a loud, lusty moan ripped out of her. Aubrey continued to lick at her clit all the way through, until Selina's hips settled onto the bed.

Slowly, Selina came back to earth, the sheets mussed around her. Droplets of sweat tickled as they glided down her cheek and arm. Her boots were heavy as they dug into the mattress. She blinked her eyes open to the sight of Aubrey pulling away, her lips swollen and glossed with Selina's juices. Lust shot through her so hot that her core ached.

"Fuck, where'd you learn to eat pussy like that?" Selina drawled, reaching down to grab Aubrey's hand and guide her up onto the bed with her.

Aubrey hovered above her, a grin lingering on her lips. "Practice."

Selina arched a brow. "You're not the only one who's had practice, sunshine. Either you take those jeans off, or I'll enjoy peeling them off you."

Aubrey reached for the button on her jeans and hesitated. "You know, I don't think I did my job yet. You're still coherent."

"There's plenty of time to addle my mind, but I've been patient, and I want my turn," Selina responded. Even as Aubrey unzipped her jeans and slid the fabric down her legs, Selina sensed a beat of hesitation that hadn't been there when she'd been on the opposite end.

She pursed her lips. "Unless you don't like

getting eaten out? I'm willing to do whatever with you, babe."

Aubrey trailed her tongue over her lips as she looked at Selina. "Damn, woman, are you psychic? Look, I'm... complicated. Truth be told, half the time I fake an orgasm just to make the girl I'm with feel decent."

Selina leaned forward, dragging Aubrey's pants down the rest of the way and guiding her onto the bed. She unzipped her boots and wriggled out of her skirt, which was in the way at this point. Selina ditched her tunic and bra next. Aubrey sat before her in panties and a crop top, a look of vulnerability on her features Selina could guarantee no one else had seen before.

Selina grabbed her hands and looked her in the eyes. "None of the faking shit with me. My ego can take it. What do you like?"

"Penetration's the only thing that gets me off, and even then, it takes a while," Aubrey admitted. "Most of the women I sleep with are satisfied with getting eaten out until their knees are jelly, and then we go our separate ways."

The thought of how lonely it had to be living a half-life and never getting the chance to be real with partners plucked at Selina's heart.

"Well, we've got one more day of vacation after this, so it's better I know your preferences now. And screw the martyr shit. Watching your partner get off is one of the things that makes the whole experience even hotter, believe me. I'm determined to see you unravel, Aubrey Moore." Selina tugged at her hand, bringing them both onto the mattress. She hooked her fingers under her crop top and yanked it up and over. Aubrey's black bra looked stunning against her tan skin and killer hips, but she wanted to see her tits far more.

Selina reached around to undo her bra, and as Aubrey tossed it over the side of the bed, Selina was already pulling on the waistband of her boy shorts, drawing them down those toned, luscious legs.

She took a moment to look at the gorgeous woman lying in front of her. Aubrey's hair was pulled back in a ponytail, the dark strands streaked with gold, and her smooth skin and defined curves begged to be bitten. Her breasts were two perfect globes, each of them a generous handful, her areolas dark and the tips of her nipples stiff. The sloping lines of her hips and the grooves of those abs drew Selina's gaze down to the thatch of curls gracing her pussy.

"Damn, you're beautiful," she purred as she

closed the distance between them. Selina pressed a kiss to Aubrey's lips, savoring the tart flavor of her own juices there. She could taste all the raw realness that spilled from them tonight. Selina had never found Aubrey more entrancing than she did in this moment, and she hadn't been lying—she didn't want a show. She wanted to watch the real Aubrey Moore unravel before her.

Selina continued kissing Aubrey as she explored her body with her fingers. Aubrey grabbed her nape in one hand and rested the other along the curve of her waist, a secure hold Selina adored. The lazy strokes of their kisses intensified the heat between them, and Selina found herself aching for Aubrey just as much as she had at the start of this.

Selina swept her hand around one breast, squeezing the velvet skin tightly. She brushed her thumb across one taut nipple and enjoyed the way Aubrey's hips bucked toward her. She tried the movement again, teasing the nipple with soft strokes and light pinches. Aubrey shuddered, and Selina filed those reactions away for later use. She continued to draw her fingers down across Aubrey's flat stomach and along the jut of her hips.

When Selina brought the pads of her fingertips

against the folds of Aubrey's pussy, the curls were soaked. She didn't go too high, avoiding the clit. If it was uncomfortable, playing around with the tender nub wouldn't be pleasurable—and she was determined to watch this woman surrender. Selina slipped two fingers between her folds, the motion deliberate. Aubrey sucked in a sharp breath as Selina glided her fingers up through her core.

"You okay?" Selina asked, murmuring against her mouth.

Aubrey nodded. "I will be."

A moment later, their arms entangled as Aubrey slid her hand down to cup Selina's pussy. She slipped her fingers inside her just as fast, and a grin lifted her lips. "Why don't we both have fun during this."

Selina fought her smile as she began to pump her fingers inside Aubrey. The woman shifted her hips back in response, but apart from the heavy breaths, she wasn't where she needed to be yet. Selina continued what she was doing, enjoying the fullness as Aubrey thrust her fingers through her in tandem. She pulled away from the languid kisses they shared and brought her lips to Aubrey's neck instead.

The moment her lips pressed there, the woman's

breathing quickened. Selina restrained her grin as she pushed into her harder, beginning to lick and suck along her neck. Aubrey's fingers continued to move inside her, each thrust easing the ache in her core. The headiness of her desire stole Selina away as she bit Aubrey's neck a little deeper and rougher than she normally would. A low moan escaped Aubrey's lips.

Selina continued to suck and bite Aubrey's neck, increasing the rhythm that she kept up inside her. Aubrey's hips bucked against her hand now, her breaths coming in sharp puffs near her ear. The low moans exploded from her more and more, and Selina savored all of it, the slick feel of her pussy, the way their breasts crushed together, and the sharp scent of lemon and sage wrapping around her, intensifying all that desire.

Each time Aubrey pumped her fingers in deep, sparks flooded through her, and fuck, Selina was close. Her sensitive clit brushed against skin, the sensation bringing her nearer to an imminent explosion. One more thrust of those strong fingers had her insides quaking a moment later, and Selina's mind blanked as she tumbled into oblivion again. She sank her teeth into Aubrey's shoulder as she rode through the intensity of the sensations.

Aubrey let out another low moan, and even through her orgasm, Selina didn't stop thrusting her fingers inside the woman. She bit even harder as her body was wrung out like a sponge, all tension released. Her breaths came out sharp and desperate as she pulled back for a breath. Aubrey's eyes were glazed, her mouth opened in soft pants, and a subtle flush spread over her cheeks.

As Selina came back to earth, she whispered her lips along Aubrey's neck, thrusting in hard and fast strokes as she brought the woman closer and closer. Aubrey slipped her fingers from Selina, and this time, she bucked her hips forward faster, as if trying to chase her own escape.

Selina sank her teeth down on Aubrey's shoulder again, thrusting deep with her fingers. A gasp flew from her lips, and a moment later, Selina could feel her pussy quaking around her fingers as Aubrey gripped her tight, their breasts crushed together. Fuck, she could explore her for hours. Aubrey's whole body stiffened for a moment until she crashed back down and relaxed completely onto the bed.

Selina took her time bringing her fingers out of Aubrey before she brought them to her lips to lick the tips. The woman tasted like honeyed sweetness. Aubrey stared at her, cheeks flushed, chest heaving, and a sheen of sweat covering every inch of her body. Selina couldn't help but slide her body flush against Aubrey's as she leaned in for another kiss. She loved how the other woman felt curved around her, their limbs fitting together like the notches of a key into a tumbler.

"That... was unreal," Aubrey murmured, stroking the side of Selina's face in a tender motion.

"Maybe there's a perk to being with someone who knows you," Selina responded, offering a half smile. Truth be told, even past exes hadn't understood her this well, and the realization was a bit dizzying.

Aubrey shook her head and pressed a tender kiss to her lips. "You're underestimating yourself again, sweetheart. That magic... that was all you."

No, it had been the two of them together, the connection that resounded more powerfully than a midsummer storm.

Selina coaxed Aubrey's lips to hers again, continuing to run her hands along the stunning body tangled up with hers. Every time the woman touched her, it sent a thrill roaring through her, whether it was a soft, tender sweep of the fingertips or the way Aubrey tightened her grip around Selina's hips. This woman got her so revved up she forgot to breathe.

Aubrey kissed her back, those languid kisses a melody Selina wanted to memorize.

"How about we make some more magic, sunshine," Selina purred in Aubrey's ear. "We've got all night."

CHAPTER FIFTEEN

THE FINAL DAY FLEW BY IN A HAZE OF KISSING, fucking, and eating the Chinese takeout they'd ordered at midday when they both realized they were starving. Aubrey couldn't think of a better way to spend the end of her vacation than with this woman.

Even amid all the bliss, Aubrey's gut still twisted at the way they'd be leaving things tonight. After she'd spilled her guts on the asphalt last night, she'd never expected Selina to invite her upstairs. Part of her had been hoping to leave this open-ended—as if she could indulge in the fantasy of coming home to someone this clever, comfortable, and intoxicating every day. Of Selina being the only one in her bed from here on out.

But Selina had set her boundaries. They were over once their vacation ended, which was now a mere four hours away. Aubrey would be driving home late tonight and then in the morning she'd head to Christiana Hospital.

Aubrey flopped onto her stomach in Selina's bed, which had gotten beyond mussed. The cool sheets caressed her bare skin since she hadn't bothered putting a stitch on today. They'd slept for a little while last night, curled up together in a way that made her feel cinnamon roll sweet, a softness washing over her like early morning light.

"I'm pretty sure chicken fried rice lasts in room temp awhile, right?" She glanced at Selina who strolled back and forth across the room holding her container of veggie lo mein. The woman wore nothing but a thong and looked like Aubrey's every fantasy come to life. Her short stature accentuated all her curves even more, from her round tits to the sloping hips that Aubrey found herself obsessed with. That ass belonged on a statue, and she'd happily spend time fucking this woman doggy style for the view alone.

If only they had more time.

Selina arched a brow, stopping mid-pace. "I'm

pretty sure chicken does not. My vegetables, on the other hand, will be doing just fine."

Aubrey lifted a forkful of food to her lips, chewed, and swallowed. "Going to take care of me when I end up sick from this?"

"You wish, sunshine," Selina said. "I'm a big fan of folks learning lessons from their actions."

Aubrey's heart thudded a little harder every time she used that nickname. Selina set her lo mein down on the dresser and sauntered over to Aubrey's side of the bed. Aubrey handed over her carton of chicken fried rice, which at this point was almost finished.

The woman moved with a mesmerizing grace, and after witnessing the way she moaned, how her toes curled during orgasm, and how she arched her back in response to touch, Aubrey was smitten. Every aspect of Selina Beckett fascinated her. She was the sort of complex painting Aubrey could spend a lifetime trying to dissemble brushstroke by brushstroke. Her gaze slipped to the digital clock on the bedstand. All the time they had was four hours and counting. The sun already set, and every minute brought them closer to departure.

Selina settled on the bed beside her and glanced at the clock too. "We'll just have to make the most of the time we've got," she said, her voice growing hushed. It was as if Selina could read her mind. Aubrey's throat tightened. She hated this. The end of vacation was bittersweet enough, but now it signaled the end of the closest thing she'd had to a relationship in five years.

How sad was her life that a weeklong summer fling fit the bill?

Not like she could blame anyone but herself.

Aubrey turned on her side to survey the woman before her. This entire room smelled like Selina's perfume, the orange blossom and amber that would probably haunt her for months afterward. She'd found Selina gorgeous for years, but nothing compared to the details she'd come to memorize about the woman lying before her. Her button nose, the pronounced dip of her collarbone, her hips, and the couple of dark moles dotting her right arm—every single aspect added another dimension to Selina Beckett.

Aubrey reached out to skim her fingers along the curve of Selina's face. "Come here, sweetheart. Ride my face."

"Why, Aubrey Moore, I thought you'd never ask," Selina responded, her eyes dancing with amusement. She slipped the waistband of her thong down her thighs, the movements slow and tantalizing.

Aubrey couldn't help but watch, growing soaked at the sight. Fuck, she'd come more at the hands of this woman in one day than she had in years. Selina operated on next-level intuition in the bedroom that someone would have to be crazy to pass up.

Aubrey didn't want to do that, honestly, but tomorrow her life would change, and she refused to make promises she couldn't keep.

Aubrey settled on her back, bringing her full focus to the beautiful woman before her. If they'd only get these moments, she didn't want to waste a single one. Selina climbed on top of her hips and took a seat, thighs pressing around her on either side.

Aubrey gave her a knowing glance. "I'll need you a bit higher if you want to enjoy this."

Selina's lips quirked. "I don't know. I'm enjoying the vantage point plenty."

Aubrey settled her hands around Selina's thighs and with a powerful jerk, pulled her closer. Selina climbed up, knees pressing in the bed as she hovered above her. Her relaxed strands were disheveled, and her tawny skin glowed under the amber lamp lights. Those gorgeous thighs on either side of her and the view of Selina's hot-as-fuck pussy was perfect. Aubrey's own pussy throbbed as Selina lowered herself down. Aubrey gripped her ass, sinking her fingers into the supple muscles. Fuck, this woman got her so turned on.

She leaned up to take a tentative first lick, sliding her tongue along those dripping folds. When Selina's arms started to tremble, Aubrey increased her speed and pressure. She aimed higher, toward her sensitive clit. She enjoyed the way Selina's breaths increased and how her chest heaved in response to the sensation. Aubrey continued to thrum her tongue along Selina's folds, flicking its tip at her clit over and over again.

From this position, she could easily devour the woman while controlling the tilt of her hips. Selina had never looked hotter, those tits on full display, her sinful ass in Aubrey's palms and her head tilted back in surrender. Each moan grew louder and louder, the sound reverberating through the air. Aubrey sank into the haze of how much she ached inside at the sight of her, sharp pleasure-pain piercing through each time she licked Selina's pussy and the woman trembled. Her legs full-out shook at this point, but Aubrey didn't cease her strokes in the slightest.

She nipped and sucked at Selina's swollen clit, which had gotten far too much attention over the past twenty-four hours. That technique pushed Selina right over the edge. Her breath caught in her throat as her whole body seized up from the force of her orgasm. Her thighs tightened on either side of Aubrey's face, her ass clenching as she came. When Selina's body relaxed, she brought her palms down on either side of Aubrey, her chest rising and falling with punctuated breaths. Selina scooted down until her lips met Aubrey's in another kiss, as if they hadn't shared thousands at this point.

Still, Aubrey couldn't get enough of the smoky, seductive taste, or of the feel of this woman. She couldn't remember a time when she'd felt this smitten.

When Selina pulled back from the kiss, her lips curled into a grin. "Knocking me breathless again, Moore." The words came out husky, but the gravity behind them couldn't be hidden. As she stared into Selina's umber eyes at the softness and the yearning there, she felt like she was submerged in the ocean and a riptide had yanked her away from solid ground. Around this woman, she was just drowning, drowning, drowning.

"Come on now," Selina said, rolling off to nudge her in the side. "I'm keeping score here. Your turn. On your hands and knees, sunshine."

Goddamn, this woman. Normally Aubrey clutched onto control like a steering wheel in a snowstorm, but around Selina, she melted into surrender every time. Somehow, she trusted her, more than she'd allowed herself to trust almost anyone in a long, long time. Aubrey pushed onto her side and pivoted to her hands and knees. Her mind reeled with the thrill of the unknown—one thing she'd come to discover in the past day was how damn inventive Selina was in bed.

She glanced back to see Selina kneeling behind her, their bodies a whisper apart. Selina ran her hands down Aubrey's thighs, the simple touch sending a thrill cascading through her entire body.

"You look so damn hot like that," she murmured, her lips quirking in a grin. She let out a puff of breath, this time drawing her nails up the insides of Aubrey's thighs. If she was turned on before, it was nothing compared to now. Her legs shook from the delicious sensation, and her nipples ached, the pointed tips taut with desire. She could feel the moistness pooling between her folds. Aubrey was bare to Selina like this, vulnerable in a way she rarely allowed herself.

Selina raked her nails along the insides of Aubrey's thighs again. Aubrey's fingers curled into the sheets in front of her as she focused all of her willpower on remaining upright. Selina gave a light push to her upper back, sending her down to her elbows. Her other hand circled her ass. She slapped Aubrey's right cheek with the sort of sting that made her pussy pulse.

"God, I need you to fuck me," Aubrey gasped out, her voice desperate. Her forehead pressed into the sheets, and she braced herself as Selina swiped her fingers between her folds. Aubrey could feel her spreading the moisture along the seams. Within moments, the woman had thrust her two fingers in all the way, her other hand resting on Aubrey's ass. Slowly, Selina began to pump her fingers inside her. White, hot sparks flew from Aubrey's fingertips to her toes, and the moans slipped from her lips unabashed.

Her entire body buzzed. Aubrey was so turned on by each movement, every glide of Selina's fingers deep inside bringing her closer and closer. Her body had never felt this sensitized before, this attuned to someone's touch, but Selina worked magic with her fingers, her tongue, and her teeth, every time. When she was here in this bed, Aubrey could let go, and she didn't know if she'd ever find bliss like this again.

As Selina thrust harder, she leaned in against her to reach around, brushing the fingertips of her free hand over Aubrey's nipple. The sensation was electric, like tiny lightning bolts arcing through her. Selina pinched her nipple, not ceasing the rhythm of her fingers, and Aubrey almost came on the spot. Selina's legs brushed against hers, the silk of her skin, the scent of sweat between them, and the inexorable heat all bringing her closer and closer.

So many times in the past, she had to grit her teeth and deal when women tried to do clit play even though it never quite felt comfortable. After one conversation with Selina, she veered into best-sex-of-her-life territory. The woman made her dream in a way she hadn't allowed herself to for a long time.

Aubrey bucked back in time to Selina's powerful thrusts, sweat prickling on her forehead as her breaths snagged in her throat. Selina moved from teasing her nipple to grabbing her breast, and then sliding her palm along her waist until she was gripping her hips tightly. Each thrust caused her to blink back stars, and she was so close to coming she could scream. An addictive tension mounted inside her, one Aubrey wanted more and more of. Her mind swirled until all she could focus on was riding Selina's fingers as her elbows and nails dug into the sheets, droplets of sweat blurring her eyes.

Selina thrust in deep, deeper, until she couldn't

hold back any longer. Aubrey's pussy pulsed around her fingers as she careened over the edge.

Sheer bliss radiated through her as her vision blanked out, her whole body floating with this intense high. Aubrey's thighs trembled, and her forehead stuck to the sheets, coated in sweat as she let out a shaky breath that she hadn't realized she'd held. Aubrey sailed on the thrill, like coursing down a lazy river until she drifted back to solid earth.

Selina pulled her fingers out of her, running her palms around her waist, her hips, her thighs, the tender caresses almost too much to bear. "Hey," Selina murmured, her voice low. "Come here, beautiful." She lowered onto the bed, leaning on her side to face Aubrey.

Aubrey slumped to the other side, their sweat-slicked bodies inches apart and their noses almost touching. Their heavy breaths mingled between them. Aubrey rested her palm on Selina's waist while Selina speared her fingers through Aubrey's hair, wild and mussed from the sheer amount of time they'd spent between the sheets today. She couldn't look away from this woman's tender gaze, finding the same thread of desperation reflected back at her.

They lay there in silence for a while, memorizing each other's features, the sound of their breaths cutting through the quiet of the room. Aubrey slid her fingertips up until she rested her hand over Selina's heart, mesmerized by the wild way it beat. How could she express the delirious elation that lifted her up every time this woman entered the room? The truth was, the words stuck in her throat, no matter how much she wanted to say more.

Her reality lay waiting in the back of her mind like the final seconds of a bomb ready to detonate. Ready to destroy any happiness she tried to grasp onto. She just surrendered to the languid touches, the taste of Selina lingering on her lips, and the heady way she felt every time they locked eyes, like they'd stumbled onto a secret oasis in the wilderness, some treasure far greater than either of them had expected.

The remaining hours ticked by in this cocoon of warmth, of bliss, of longing, until those hours turned to minutes, and the time to return to the rental arrived.

Aubrey searched around the floor for her clothes from yesterday which had been flung around and forgotten from the moment she locked herself away in Selina's room. She tugged on her underwear and ripped jeans, and snapped her bra back on. She paused, crop top in hand, as she glanced over at

Selina, who lounged on the bed wearing absolutely nothing.

"You're going to make leaving impossible," she murmured, hoping Selina didn't notice the roughness of her voice. Aubrey slung the crop top over her head before she crossed the space to kneel on the bed. She stared at her balled fists. "I don't want this to be over."

Except Selina had made her terms clear—they had until the end of their vacation, which had arrived. Aubrey couldn't even fight for the relationship if she wanted to. Not now, while Mom's health was in limbo and her whole world could come crumbling down at any moment. Who would want to start a relationship like that?

Selina's hand met hers, and their fingers intertwined. For a moment, Aubrey sat on the bed frozen in place, unwilling to move. If she just stayed here, she could keep avoiding reality. If she just stayed here, she could pretend Selina was hers.

Selina pressed her lips together, and a shadow crossed over her eyes. When she looked up and their gazes met, Aubrey swallowed. The same pain radiated there.

"Guess I'll be seeing you around, sunshine,"

Selina said, the words coming out hoarse. Aubrey felt them scrape over her bones.

She closed the distance between them, and their lips met. They'd shared hundreds of kisses, but this one twisted her insides. This one contained all of the unspoken words that weighted the air between them, every last truth she wanted to confess to this woman, every promise she wished she could make. Selina tasted sweet, the tang of her swollen lips holding Aubrey's heart captive. Her eyes pricked, and she pulled away before her emotions got the better of her.

"I'll see you back home, sweetheart," Aubrey said, pushing up off the bed. Her fingers trembled as she slipped into her shoes. She glanced at Selina one last time before reaching for the handle. "Never change, Selina Beckett."

At that, she turned the cold knob and stepped into the darkened hallway, leaving her heart behind.

CHAPTER SIXTEEN

THE NEXT MORNING WAS A PAINFUL WAKEUP. Not just because she'd had marathon sex with Aubrey for close to twenty-four hours straight, but the empty bed also reminded her that all of it had come to an end.

Cass rapped on her door. "We've got to be out of here by noon. You all ready?"

"Just grabbing my bags," Selina said, finishing tidying up the room, like the time she'd spent in bed with Aubrey was some distant dream. In fact, with the bright sunlight streaming through the windows and the sounds of her roommates bustling around downstairs, that's what it felt like.

Selina tossed on comfy clothes for the short drive back, choosing a pair of black shorts and a lacy gray tank top. She grabbed her suitcase and the red duffel bag she'd packed, skimming over the room in case she'd missed anything. The sheets were pin straight and the comforter smoothed down. The bed looked so different from the mess she and Aubrey had made of it while covered in sweat and panting. Every inch of this room now held memories of the woman, ones that would be hard to forget.

Selina should be mad at herself for the hurt and heartbreak sure to follow, but she couldn't regret the time they'd spent together.

After Kat, she'd shut herself off from so much, hesitant to put herself out there for fear of adding more slices to her already bleeding heart. With Aubrey, the eventual separation would hurt, but she dove in anyway. That had been the push Selina needed to get back out there, forcing her to realize that even if she crash-landed, she'd survive.

Selina placed her palm on the brass knob and turned, exiting her room. She could hear Cass and Steph bickering in the kitchen, arguing about left-over pizza from Sal's. A grin cracked Selina's face. She might not have spent as much time with the girls as normal, but she couldn't say she'd missed out on this vacation. The experiences with Aubrey were ones she'd carry with her for a long time to come.

Selina thumped down the steps and headed for the door. "I'm going to pack my car," she called back. "I'll be in to help with the rest."

"Fine," Steph called out, "but if you try to lay claim on these pizza leftovers, I'll end you, Beckett."

Selina snorted. "Not even a blip on my radar. Have at it, guys." She headed out to the wicker-furniture-covered front porch, her throat squeezing tight. All she could see was the dozens of times Aubrey had made some excuse to interrupt her while she was reading. She'd been blind not to realize the banter between them would erupt in a fiery conclusion.

She strode down the steps toward her green Subaru and popped the trunk. Selina loaded the suitcases in one at a time, trying to stave off fears about the future, of the first time Aubrey tried to pick up someone in her bar and she'd be the bystander as always. She couldn't keep clinging to fear as an excuse to hide away from the world though.

She heaved a sigh as she slammed the trunk down. Selina leaned against the back of her car and pulled out a cigarette, lighting the end. The first blissful drag of nicotine coursed through her.

A grunt sounded from the house next door. Kyle stepped into view, hauling a duffel bag over her shoulder as she brought it to rest on the back of a car.

The redhead's chin-length hair obscured her face from view a moment, but based on the slick of sweat along her arms, she'd been toting luggage for a bit.

Kyle glanced at her and grinned. "Last one." She hooked her fingers through the belt loops of her jean shorts and sauntered over.

Selina sucked in another drag of her cigarette and let the smoke pour out, aiming it away from Kyle. The woman halted in front of her.

"So," Kyle said, glancing at her feet. "You and Aubrey?"

Selina swallowed hard. Damn, this would be harder than she thought. "Yeah, for the trip only."

Kyle let out a low swear. "That woman, I swear, I'm going to wring her neck. You're the first person I've seen her open up to besides me and Sky, and the only one she's expressed any romantic interest in." Kyle glanced at her with an apologetic wince. "I'm sorry. I'm rubbing salt in the wound here, right?"

Selina shook her head, letting out another stream of smoke, as if she stood a chance at steadying her nerves. "I set the limit, not her. The situation with her mom had her in such a tailspin that I knew I'd never get the answer I wanted." She shrugged. "I'm a big girl. I know how to pick up my own pieces." Even as she said that, her heart throbbed with a choking intensity. The week she'd spent with Aubrey had illustrated everything she'd wanted in a relationship —the comfort of knowing how to respond, the constant teasing, and the genuine connection she'd searched ages for.

Of course she fell for the woman who could never commit.

"She never actually called it quits?" Kyle asked, her tone sharpening.

"None of the meddling shit," Selina responded, arching a brow. "I set the limit to keep from being hurt more, not so I could linger on false hopes."

"Right, right," Kyle said, spearing her fingers through her strands. "She said her goodbyes last night before she darted home."

"She was going to visit her mom in the hospital this morning," Selina murmured. Even though they'd ended things, she couldn't help worrying about Aubrey right now. The woman tried to toss on a tough exterior for everyone else, but it'd been clear to Selina from the first day of this vacation that Aubrey'd been hurting for a long while.

Kyle's brows drew together. "Her mom? I thought she was out of the hospital."

"Went back in again a few days ago," Selina responded. Aubrey might not want them to know, but if Selina couldn't be there, she could at least ensure her closest would be.

"Christ, I'm going to kill that woman," Kyle muttered, scrubbing her face. "No wonder she's been acting dodgy the past few days. There's no way we're leaving her to deal with that by her lonesome." Kyle glanced at her. "Thanks, Selina. If I could ever get my best friend's head out of her ass, I wouldn't want to see her with anyone but you."

Selina nodded, trying to ignore the shaky wave of emotion that crashed through her. She took a final drag from her cigarette and crushed it under foot. "Good luck, Kyle. I'll see you next time you're at Renegades."

Kyle saluted her and jogged off toward her rental. Selina sucked in a breath of the salt air, wishing it could cleanse all the worries and doubts away. She knew she'd survive—she had to. But even now, her heart ached at the thought of Aubrey.

She'd never planned on falling, but somewhere between the first walk on the beach and the way Aubrey cracked her past wide open last night, it had happened.

She headed back up the steps to the porch, returning to help with the rest of the cleanup. Her heart ached, not with regret, but the loss of something so beautiful and powerful that she doubted she'd ever glimpse it again. With a swallow, she settled her hand on the doorknob.

Vacation had come to a close. Time to return to reality.

CHAPTER SEVENTEEN

T**HE** **SCENT** **OF** **DISINFECTANT** **AND** **DECAY** assaulted her senses once she entered the hospital. Aubrey avoided the place at all costs because it reminded her far too much of this—coming to find out if her mom's condition had worsened.

She'd arrived the moment visiting hours opened. Chels had texted her asking to be filled in on any results. They should be coming in today.

Aubrey walked down the glaringly white corridor, the fluorescent lights burning into her, bleaching out her skin and spirit. Leaving Selina last night had torn what little bit of her remained, and this place just threatened continued torture. Bile rose in her throat as she closed in on Mom's room number. Fuck, she should've brought flowers, chocolates, or some sort of token to prove she wasn't a negligent daughter. Not like Dad would've let her visit earlier in the week. He could be so damn stubborn, one trait she wished she hadn't gotten from him.

Aubrey balled her hands into fists that she released, and then did it again and again and again. The numbers ticked down like a countdown she wasn't prepared for. She sucked in a deep breath, trying to steady herself against the muddle of fears and doubts threatening to seize her limbs. Mom needed her strong, not ready to bawl her eyes out.

Room 309 stood out in front of her.

Showtime.

Aubrey peeked in, holding onto the doorframe. There were two beds in the room, one empty. Mom lay in the one closest to the door, a Nora Roberts book in hand. Aubrey clutched the frame even tighter. Mom didn't look too pale, even though the washed-out blue nightgown she wore didn't do her any favors. Her rumpled brown hair was pulled into a ponytail, and her lips were bare of her usual crimson lipstick.

"Hey, Mama," Aubrey said, rapping the side of the doorway before she entered.

Mom's head snapped up, and her eyes crinkled. "My girl. I'm guessing your sister told you?"

Aubrey strode over to her, her hand balled into a fist so tight the nails bit into her palms. "Why didn't you say anything? I would've come back in a heartbeat."

Mom reached out and wrapped a hand around her fist. "That's why. Because you would've rushed home from your vacation when my life wasn't in danger. I don't know what Chelsea told you, but I wasn't on death's door. Two fainting spells aren't going to kill a cancer survivor, honey."

Aubrey's fist loosened, and she slipped her hand in her mom's, holding tight. "You say that, but we almost lost you, Mama. What if the fainting spells are a sign of the cancer coming back?"

"That's what we addressed first," Mom said, looking her in the eyes. Her palm was warm, and the faint scent of cinnamon cut through the sterile smell of this place. "It's not cancer. Your sister was worried they'd made a mistake and wanted me to test again, but I know it's not."

"How can you be sure though?" Aubrey jumped in, agreeing with her sister. So many times she'd heard stories of cancer survivors living regular lives until that illness crept in again to come and claim them. She'd scrolled through far too many horror stories in the forums, and they'd left an imprint.

Mom shook her head, a soft smile on her lips. "I know you're all just scared it'll return, but trust me. The results came in today. I've developed late onset diabetes, but some abnormalities in the test kept them from being able to assess what was going on. Plus, they had your father shouting in their ear about cancer the whole time."

Aubrey's mouth dropped open. "So, it's not cancer?"

Relief distributed a swift uppercut, knocking the breath from her.

Not cancer.

Mom smiled, the wrinkles in her face warm and soft. "This is why I didn't want to say anything until we had answers, honey. Not because we didn't want you to know, but because it was pointless worrying until we could confirm what was going on. I wish I could've kept you and Chelsea from the panic you must've gone through during all of this. You've both dealt with enough already."

"So...," Aubrey said, trying to ignore how her eyes were glossed with liquid. "Diabetes, right? All sugar-free stuff from here on out. Heard it makes you shit your brains out."

Mom gave her a pointed look. "I'll observe a diet and follow protocols, but you can bet I'm sneaking sugar once in a while. Just don't tell your father." Mom squeezed her hand, and Aubrey let out a shaky breath, managing to hold back her tears.

"But you're going to be okay," Aubrey said, almost disbelieving that things might turn out good for once, especially after the rainstorm of worries that plagued her all week.

"As much as any of us can be," Mom responded. The words were familiar and worn, ones she'd used again and again when Chelsea and Aubrey hovered over the woman during the chemo treatments. Her knowing gaze landed on Aubrey, and she was defenseless. "Sweetheart, you don't need to put your life on hold, even if I do get sick. You haven't brought around anyone since Lila, and I'm not blind. I know why."

Aubrey swallowed. Her mother would see right through any attempt to lie. "People aren't as reliable as you want them to be," she murmured, casting her glance to the floor.

"Some aren't," Mom said, reaching out to squeeze her hand. "But others stick with you through anything. You're proof positive of that."

Aubs chewed on her lip, trying to ignore the heat welling in her eyes. Her phone buzzed in her pocket.

Aubrey pulled it out, desperate for a distraction. She glanced at the screen. Kyle had texted.

We're in Christiana. What room?

Goddamnit. She hadn't said anything, but those considerate fuckers somehow figured her situation out.

"Apparently Kyle's here," Aubrey said, letting out a shaky sigh. "Do you mind if I go find her to tell her everything's okay? I'll be right back."

"Take your time," Mom said, letting go of her hand. "I was getting to the good part of the chapter."

Aubrey shook her head, unable to help the wry grin lifting her lips. She shot a text off to Kyle telling her to stay put and that she'd meet them at the entrance. The sight of her mom lying there with her thick book cracked open caused her mind to drift to the other woman in her life who constantly buried her nose in one. The stunner she'd left behind in Rehoboth. Her heart twisted, despite the relief.

In all her years of hopping from bed to bed, Selina was her one regret.

If she had any sense in her, she would've made the woman her girlfriend before the week ended. A rare gem like Selina Beckett was worth holding onto.

Aubrey power walked her way to the elevator,

moving as fast as possible to get to the lobby. Her heart throbbed in her ears.

The cancer hadn't returned.

Mom was going to be okay.

The elevator creaked open, and right as she got in, the doors slid shut behind her. The ding, ding, ding of the floors echoed in the confined space, but she stared at the ceiling, feeling a strange combination of elated and heartbroken. She'd only ever feel relief about the news about her mother, but it came on the tails of the best week she'd experienced with another woman, one who she'd let walk away.

She stepped out onto the main floor, and it took her a few seconds to spot Kyle standing there with Mia and Sky. Aubrey slowed her pace, embarrassment flushing through her that she'd gotten so worked up and dragged her friends into her worries. Fuck, she needed to text Chels the good news. All of the adrenaline that had been coursing through her on the way to the hospital room cracked inside her like an egg, leaving her jittery in the aftermath.

"Hey guys," Aubrey said, slipping her hands into her pockets as she approached.

Ky bounded up and threw her arms around her. "You idiot. Stop leaving us out in the cold."

Aubrey buried her head in the crook of Ky's

neck, trying to hide the tears that trickled out. Her best friend just held her tighter. "Sorry, Ky," she murmured, her voice growing thick. "She's okay though. She's going to be okay."

"I'm glad," Ky murmured, not breaking the hug. Aubrey's breaths evened, and her tears imprinted on Ky's skin, ceasing as fast as they began. With a shaky breath, she pulled away from Ky and stepped over, opening her arms to both Mia and Sky, who swarmed in for a hug. The warmth flooded through her like an expanding bubble had burst. She'd trust these women with her life.

When she finally pulled back from their embrace, Aubs wiped her eyes, trying to hide any further evidence of her emotional reaction. A small grin played on Ky's lips at the sight.

"How did you guys figure out she was back in the hospital?" Aubrey asked. She took a seat in one of the lobby chairs, needing to steady herself.

Sky and Mia took seats in the chairs beside Aubrey, but Ky kept standing. Her brows drew together. "Selina told me. And I know right now might not be the time...," her best friend started to say and stopped.

Aubrey shrugged. "I fucked up, okay? Yeah, she's a keeper, and she's the one woman who's made me feel anything in years, but the trip was our one time together. She made the call, not me, and I need to respect it."

"That's a load of horseshit," Sky said, glancing over at her. Aubrey stuck up her middle finger in response.

Ky crouched in front of her, looking up with those serious hazel eyes. She grabbed Aubrey's hands in hers. "I saw her before we left. She made the call to protect herself because you never staked any claims. That's not the sort of woman you walk away from. I'm invoking the Rehoboth Pact, Aubs."

A bitter laugh flew from her lips. Earlier this year she'd been in a similar position, smacking sense into Sky when she was about to walk away from the best relationship in her life. Aubs squeezed Ky's hands and shook her head.

When they'd made the Pact those years back, she'd felt so hopeless. It had been the lighthouse in the storm she'd clung to all this time, that if she ever found the one and fucked the chance up, her friends would call her out.

Well, the Rehoboth Pact had just been invoked, here in the middle of Christiana's lobby.

"You're too good for me, Kyle Walker." Aubrey sank deeper into the hard plastic seat. "But seriously.

I haven't been in a committed relationship in years—I'm probably garbage at it, and no one deserves to struggle through that, least of all Selina." Even as she protested, hope flickered in her chest like an incandescent bulb.

"Enough excuses, Aubs." Sky squeezed Mia's shoulder. "If you hadn't invoked it for me, I might've passed up on this. I've never seen you fall for someone before in all the time I've known you. But what's between you and Selina? That's the real deal."

Aubrey's heart pounded hard. Could she actually do this? Would she even last five seconds in a relationship?

Every time she thought about Selina Beckett, her heart wanted to say yes.

"I'll beat you up if you don't go for this," Kyle threatened, even though her lips kept tugging into a grin.

The dam in Aubrey's chest broke, all those worries just cascading over her along with every secret hope she'd ever clung onto. The hopes won out. "Out of fear of fighting Kyle alone, I'll do it," she murmured. "I'll be at Renegades tonight. You can all make sure I don't back out on this one. Now go home and get some rest. I promised my mother some quality time while she's holed up in the hospital."

Kyle squeezed her hands again and rose, a genuine grin lighting her features. "We'll be there. Give your mom an extra hug from me." At that, Sky and Mia rose from their seats as well, and the three started heading for the door.

"Will do," Aubrey called, tipping two fingers in a salute. She headed toward the elevators, her mind swirling with hundreds of possibilities.

Selina might turn her down after all of this. She might've fucked up her chances for good with the one woman she'd let in.

But Aubrey had been spinning on this shitty teacup ride for years now. It was high time she got off and stepped onto stable ground. She couldn't back out now, even if she wanted to. Kyle and Sky had invoked the Rehoboth Pact, an agreement she viewed as sacred.

Tonight, she would confess everything she'd been holding back.

She only hoped Selina felt the same way.

CHAPTER EIGHTEEN

The buzz of Renegades settled over Selina's skin. It was the home she'd created for herself. The hibiscus wreaths she'd made hung from the windows, and amid the rich scents of wood and porter, she caught the faint thread of herbs, something she always adored about this place. Coming home felt bittersweet after the transcendent vacation she had, but she found comfort in sinking back into routine as well.

Her skin was still tingling, and her heart was thumping faster than normal, but the sight of her bar drew her in, a tether of real life she sorely needed.

The crowd wasn't too bustling right now, which worked perfectly for her return home. The after-dinner rush was when things would surge and get chaotic. Her barback Mina would be in by then though, and she hoped the woman's training hadn't lapsed in her time away. Heather ran a tidy ship with minimal fires to put out upon return, but Selina'd be spending the next few days holed away with all the paperwork she needed to catch up on.

She couldn't help how her gaze kept slipping to the door, as if she expected Aubrey Moore to walk through. She both longed for and dreaded the moment.

A gorgeous brunette sat down on an open stool and ordered a gin and tonic, so Selina set about preparing the drink. Even after a week away, the motions were mechanical, a muscle memory she hadn't lost. Within a minute, she set the fresh drink on the counter in front of the woman.

Selina glanced up.

Aubrey strode in through the front door.

The woman looked stunning like always, her hair pulled into a ponytail and a glow to her sepia skin like she carried the sunshine in with her. She wore a skintight racerback shirt and red shorts that hugged her muscular ass. At once, Selina's heart forgot to take a cue and picked up speed. The intense time they'd spent kissing and fucking failed in getting the woman out of her system. If anything, it made her want to hop over the bar, wrap her arms around her, and drink in the scent of lemon and sage. Selina just needed to feel that lithe body pressed against hers.

She worked her jaw. Restraint. The thing she needed badly right now. She grabbed a glass, pretending to polish it with a rag if only to give her something to focus on.

Aubrey marched right up to the bar in front of her.

"Hey," Aubrey said, spreading her palms on the counter. "We need to talk."

Selina's internal alarms clanged, but by some miracle she maintained a level face. "In case you didn't notice, I'm working right now." Which meant she also couldn't have a breakdown on the floor in case the talk with Aubrey went south.

Aubrey crossed her arms and took a seat on the stool. "When are you off?" Her gaze sparked with challenge, a look promising trouble. Selina wasn't sure if she wanted to scream or run the other way.

"I've got a break in a half hour when Mina gets here," Selina offered, which was the best she could do. At least then she could have her breakdown in private once all of this came crashing down.

Aubrey settled onto her stool and offered a brazen grin. "Excellent. Then I'll wait."

Selina sucked in a breath, her sanity like the last drips from a keg ready to kick. Just yesterday, they'd been entwined in each other's arms, reaching the heights of a perfection she'd never experienced. The sex had been out of this world, but beyond that, the closeness, the way she'd come to understand Aubrey, and how they both seemed to melt around each other was brand-new. If Aubrey didn't give her space, she'd never be able to cleanse herself of all the hopes she'd attached to their time together.

"What can I get you to drink?" Selina asked.

"You should know at this point," Aubrey shot back, pure sass.

Selina's hands moved on their own as she grabbed the rum and poured it into the glass she'd been polishing. The coke came next, and then she was handing the drink over to Aubrey, working on automatic. Her heart pounded in her ears, louder and louder and louder.

They'd agreed last night would be it. So why was Aubrey Moore sitting in her bar staring at her with the same sort of swoony looks she'd given while they were on vacation? She shook her head as she set the drink on the bar. Aubrey tried to hand over cash, but Selina turned it down.

"You want to talk, we'll talk. This is just to tide you over."

A hand waved at the end of the bar, someone signaling they needed a refill. Selina set to work, striding away from Aubrey. As she poured a refill of the Dogfish Head brew on tap, she couldn't help but notice the woman in her peripheral. She'd already begun to talk to the brunette she sat beside, animatedly chatting. Selina's stomach twisted in knots.

She should kick her out now and ban her from Renegades for good before Aubrey took a wrench to her glass heart.

New faces had begun to swing in, the beginnings of the evening crowd showing up, which kept her hands busy. She forced her smiles, words flowing from her lips that she barely paid attention to. Selina just kept on moving from one drink and one customer to the next. Aubrey still sat there chatting with the same girl, and she tried to force down the queasiness in her stomach. This was how her nightmare began as Aubrey went back to hitting on the first chick she ran into, and Selina would have to fight to forget every sweet moment they'd shared.

Her fingers felt as numb as her heart, but she continued to move on autopilot. Gin and whisky poured, beer flowed from the taps, and limes and lemons stung her fingers. She tried to focus on the faces before her, but even when she wasn't looking at Aubrey, she sensed the woman's presence on the other side of the bar, driving her insane.

If Aubrey couldn't give her the space she needed to heal, that ban might be in order. She couldn't go through nights of this, working through the pain while it paraded in front of her face.

Mina swung behind the bar, her long blonde hair swishing with the movement. She flashed a bright grin. "All set, boss. Ready to continue our training?"

Selina sucked in a breath. Now or never. "It's time for me to go on my dinner break, and then I'm all yours. The crowd here's mostly refills right now, and I'll be right out back if you need me."

Mina saluted and slid past her to find a comfortable spot to stand. Selina's throat dried as she looked in Aubrey's direction. The woman still chatted away with the brunette, and part of her wanted to march on by and ignore the two of them. She could go to grab a bite in the back in peace.

Instead, she found herself stopping in front of Aubrey. She schooled her features before she spoke "If you want to talk, I've got the time now."

Aubrey glanced at the girl she'd been talking

with. "Sorry," she said, flashing a smile. "I've got to go. My future girlfriend's here."

Selina's jaw dropped. Aubrey winked and slid off the stool, heading for the back of the house with a swing to her hips like she owned the place. Selina's legs moved on automatic as she followed her through the door. Those words resounded over and over again, ballooning inside her with a hope she could barely dare believe in. Once they stepped into the back, Selina swerved past her, heading toward the emergency exit she propped open for smoke breaks. They both stepped through the door.

Selina leaned against the brick wall, needing something solid to hold her upright. The summer air was stagnant and sticky, but she crossed her arms over her chest as she glanced at Aubrey, waiting for her to clarify why she'd shown up tonight. Aubrey paced in front of her, wringing her hands a bit, enough that Selina needed to put her out of her misery.

"How's your mom doing?" Selina asked, her voice hoarse.

Aubrey glanced up, her gaze softening. "She's got a diagnosis of diabetes, not cancer, so a lot better than we'd anticipated. But that's not why I'm here tonight. I wanted to talk about us."

Selina cocked an eyebrow, unable to offer more. Her heart thundered so loud it was a miracle she could hear anything else.

Aubrey Moore engaging in a conversation about the two of them was the last thing she'd expected.

"I know I have the worst reputation, and it's been well earned. I understand if you don't want anything to do with me, and if you want to cling to the agreement we made back in Rehoboth, I get that too." Aubrey kicked her heel against the brick wall behind her, staring down at the ground as if she couldn't bear to look up.

"But…," Selina said, her chest soaring even though she didn't have any safety measures to break the fall.

"But I want more than a vacation with you," Aubrey said, her gaze swinging up to snare Selina's. Those dark eyes percolated with unrestrained emotion. "You're everything I could want, Selina Beckett. From the secret romantic dwelling beneath all that calm to the steadiness you emanate even when I'm being a pain in the ass—you balance me in every way. And the more I got to know you, the more you awakened all this damned longing that's just about killing me."

Aubrey hesitated, but she didn't look away. "I

can't promise I'll be any good at this commitment shit—hell, it's been so long. Shit, I don't know if you can even trust me after how often you've had to deal with me coming into Renegades—"

Selina grabbed her hands, the motion cutting her off. Aubrey glanced up to meet her eyes.

"Are you saying you want something serious?" Selina asked, her lips threatening to curl into a smile.

"I'm saying I want to be with you through every-thing—birthdays, holidays, adventures, and even the bad shit," Aubrey said, a tremor in her voice. "I'm saying one week wasn't enough, Selina Beckett. I want you until the end of time, if we can dare."

The distance between them was too much, her chest pumping too hard to stand it. Selina closed in, brushing her lips against Aubrey's. Aubrey wrapped a hand around her nape and kissed her hungrily, as if they hadn't seen each other in years. Selina sank into this kiss, the one filled with all the promise she'd never dared to dream of. Aubrey tasted like rum, desire, and hope, and Selina lost herself in this woman. Her mouth coaxed out a moan from Aubrey, and she pulled away.

"If we go any further, I'm going to jump you right here in the alley," Aubrey said, her grip tight-ening on Selina's nape.

"It's my bar," Selina responded, cocking an eyebrow.

Aubrey grinned, shaking her head. "So, girlfriends?"

Selina snuck in again to nip at her bottom lip, unable to help the giddiness bubbling up inside her. "Yeah. You're all mine, Aubrey Moore. I play for keeps, and from the moment you opened up to me back at Castaways in Rehoboth, I wanted you. You're so full of life, this beautiful, reckless hurricane that smashed into my life while I tried to hide away from the world. There was no way I couldn't fall for you."

Aubrey shook her head, her eyes crinkling with how big her grin grew. "You're a once-in-a-lifetime girl, Selina Beckett. I was an idiot for almost passing this up because I was clinging to old fears. If you're willing to chance this, I'm with you all the way." Aubrey brushed her thumb along Selina's lower lip, sending sparks throughout her entire body. The tenderness in her gaze was everything she'd been hoping for.

Selina nodded, her heart thumping so hard she was surprised the cops hadn't arrived with a noise complaint. "I knew I waited for a reason," she murmured. "I just didn't realize it was you."

A flush rose to Aubrey's cheeks, and she slipped

her hand in Selina's. "As much as I want to keep making out with you here, Sky, Mia, and Kyle are waiting inside for us. I promised them I'd tell you the truth about how I felt."

"Then let's go tell the world," Selina said, gripping her hand tight as they stepped back in through the door, together.

EPILOGUE

Three months later

THE KEYS JANGLED IN AUBREY'S HAND, MAKING this a reality.

She strode up the walkway with Selina, hand in hand. The place before them was a beautiful two-story town house right near Renegades with red trim and white paneling. There was enough space inside for a workout room for Aubrey, a guest bedroom, and the one they'd be sharing.

Move in day had arrived.

Selina squeezed Aubrey's hand. "I'm glad we're taking this step."

"Well, I'm petrified," Aubrey muttered. "I haven't lived with anyone since Lila, and we all saw how spectacularly that went."

Selina nudged her in the side. "What about me makes you think I'm a vanishing in the night type? This girl wants roots, remember?"

"So they all say, until the hairdresser calls them out on their faux ombre," Aubrey shot back, trying to deflect her nerves. The past three months had been a total dream. She and Selina spent every night together, at one place or the other, and beyond the insane chemistry and extraordinary amount of time fucking, Aubrey just enjoyed coming home to someone. Selina's admission from back at the shore had lingered, and it was true how having someone to return home to, someone to brew coffee for in the morning made a difference.

So when her lease came up around the same time as Selina's, she hadn't hesitated in offering that they go in on a place together. Seemed like a great idea at the time, but the closer they got to the move-in date, the more those jitters amplified.

What if Mom got sick and Selina bailed? What if she failed at being a decent girlfriend? What if Selina's three cats hated living with her and devoured her in her sleep?

The last one was the only one she'd admitted on a regular basis, even though Selina managed to pry the other two worries from her. Each time, they'd talk it out until she landed on stable ground again. She'd never in her life met someone who grounded her like Selina did.

Aubrey stopped in front of the door, lifting her key hand. "Guess this is it."

"You realize we're entering our new place, not a funeral, right?" Selina responded, her tone dry in a way Aubrey always adored. An amused smirk hovered on her lips.

Aubrey shot her a look. "What if everything breaks on the first day and—"

Selina placed a finger over her mouth. "Turn the key, and let's step inside. Worries can take a back seat right now."

Aubrey huffed a breath against Selina's finger, the weight of their decision making her shiver. She lifted her brows. "Or we could just make out here on the doorstep for a while."

"In, sunshine," Selina commanded, pointing to the door.

"Right," Aubrey said, slipping the key into the slot. She opened the door, and the world didn't burst into flames. She took the first steps into their town house and didn't collapse into a wreck on the floor. In fact, with each step into the tan-carpeted open living room, those worries dripped to the floor like hot wax. The sunlight streamed in through the window, casting dappled beams onto the pale carpets, tiny dust motes floating through like fairies.

Selina slipped her hand in Aubrey's, standing beside her. "Hey," she said, her voice soft and filled with emotion as she nudged her in the side again. "This place is ours, babe."

Aubrey swallowed thickly as she surveyed the place before her. Even though they hadn't filled it with their things yet, she could already imagine lazy Monday nights on the couch cuddled up with Selina, fucking her against every wall in this house, and spending time in the kitchen making meals together. The more she envisioned a future here, in this place, the less terrifying it seemed.

A grin broke out on her lips, elation bubbling inside her as she squeezed Selina's hand tight.

"We're home."

Looking for more F/F romances? Check out the final book in the Rehoboth Pact series,

RESTRAINED DESIRES. Not yet read book one? Pick up **CONFINED DESIRES** today! Plus check out Katherine's M/M romance **MIDNIGHT HEIST**.

ACKNOWLEDGMENTS

Books take a village to make them shine, and I'm so grateful for the help of Jess, Amy, Fable, and Kris for their beta reading input and for my critique partners Ember Leigh and Jaqueline Snowe for their keen insight. As always, a massive thanks to everyone at Hot Tree Publishing for taking a chance on me and my stories, and my editors for helping me polish this one! You're all wonderful, and Selina and Aubrey's story wouldn't be the same without you!

ABOUT THE AUTHOR

Katherine McIntyre is a feisty chick with a big attitude despite her short stature. She writes stories featuring snarky women, ragtag crews, and men with bad attitudes—and there's an equally high chance for a passionate speech thrown into the mix. As an eternal geek and tomboy who's always stepped to her own beat, she's made it her mission to write stories that represent the broad spectrum of people out there, from different cultures and races to all varieties of men and women.

Website: http://www.katherine-mcintyre.com
Newsletter sign-up: http://eepurl.com/duIScb

facebook.com/kmcintyreauthor

twitter.com/pixierants

instagram.com/authorkmcintyre

bookbub.com/profile/katherine-mcintyre

ABOUT THE PUBLISHER

Hot Tree Publishing opened its doors in 2015 with an aspiration to bring quality fiction to the world of readers. With the initial focus on romance and a wide spread of romance subgenres, Hot Tree Publishing has since opened their first imprint, Tangled Tree Publishing, specializing in crime, mystery, suspense, and thriller.

Firmly seated in the industry as a leading editing provider to independent authors and small publishing houses, Hot Tree Publishing is the sister company to Hot Tree Editing, founded in 2012. Having established in-house editing and promotions, plus having a well-respected market presence, Hot Tree Publishing endeavors to be a leader in bringing quality stories to the world of readers.

Interested in discovering more amazing reads brought to you by Hot Tree Publishing? Head over to the website for information:

www.hottreepublishing.com

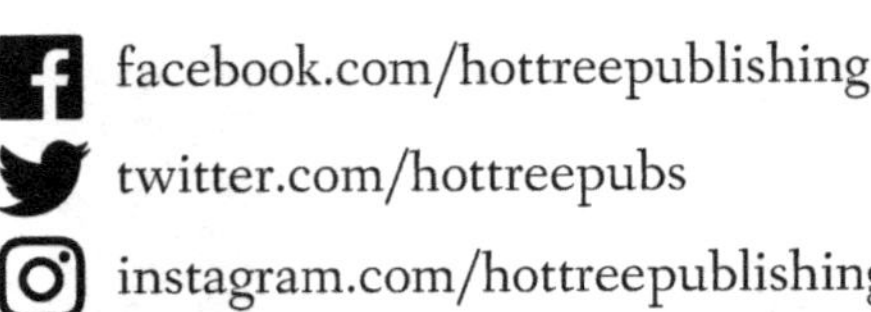

facebook.com/hottreepublishing
twitter.com/hottreepubs
instagram.com/hottreepublishing